About the Book

Soccer is the world's favorite sport, and its popularity is exploding across our country. Spurred on by the dramatic World Cup victory of America's women's team, league ranks are growing with members of all ages. The fast pace, simple rules, and accessible equipment make the game fun to watch and play no matter where you live.

All About Soccer covers basic rules, equipment, player positions, skills, and strategies; Olympic and World Cup competition; and the history of organized soccer in the United States. Star players of yesterday and today are included, as well as information about leagues for people who want to play for fun and maybe hope to become the stars of tomorrow.

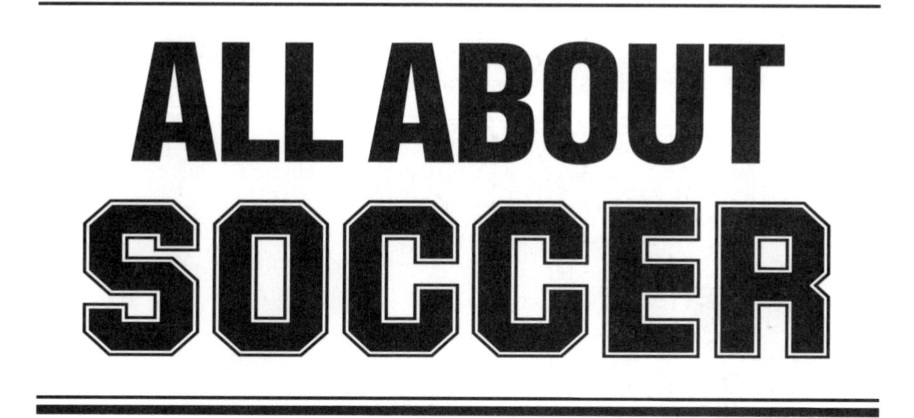

George Sullivan

Illustrated with photographs and diagrams

G. P. Putnam's Sons New York

Acknowledgments

Many people helped me in the preparation of this book, and I am grateful to them all. Special thanks are due Coach Pete McNamara, Fordham Prep School, Bronx, New York, and Coach Nola Thacker and team members Allison Chambers and Karen Cherrington of the Brooklyn Phoenix, New York Metropolitan Women's Soccer League.

—*George Sullivan, New York City*

FRONTISPIECE: Duke's Ali Curtis tracks down the ball during ACC Championship play.

FRONT COVER PHOTOGRAPH: Courtesy of World Wide Photo.
BACK COVER PHOTOGRAPH: PAM / International Sports Images.

INTERIOR PHOTOGRAPHS: Jeffrey A. Camarati of Duke University Photography, frontispiece; Columbus Crew, 100; Dartmouth College, 18; International Sports Images / J. Brett Whitesell, 3, 4, 31, 78, 81, 84, 88, 90; FIFA, 75; Furman University, 69; Indiana University, 54; Miami Fusion, 17; New York Public Library, 105; Scott Quintard / ASUCLA Photography, 22, 44, 59; Saint Louis University, 16; George Sullivan, 2, 11, 12, 13, 14, 25, 27, 29, 35, 49, 55, 56, 57, 67, 95, 97; University of Iowa, 20; University of Oklahoma, 50; University of Washington / Joan Komura, 23; Washington State University, 47, 68; Yale University, 5.

G. P. Putnam's Sons, a division of Penguin Putnam Books for Young Readers,
345 Hudson Street, New York, NY 10014. G. P. Putnam's Sons, Reg. U.S. Pat. & Tm. Off.
Published simultaneously in Canada. Printed in the United States of America.
Designed by Sharon Murray Jacobs. Text set in twelve-point New Caledonia.
Library of Congress Cataloging-in-Publication Data
Sullivan, George, 1927– All about soccer/George Sullivan. p. cm. Includes index.
1. Soccer—Juvenile literature. [1. Soccer.] I. Title. GV943.25.S93 2001 796.334—dc21
00-03905 ISBN 0-399-23481-0 (Hardcover) ISBN 0-399-23646-5 (Paperback)
3 5 7 9 10 8 6 4 2

Contents

Introduction

Soccer is the most popular game in the world. The reason is no mystery: All you need to play is a ball and a level piece of ground, and the rules are easy to understand.

You don't need a certain body type. You don't need to be tall. You don't have to be big and strong. Skill is more important than strength.

And soccer is a great equalizer. Boys don't have any physical advantage. Girls can run and kick and head the ball just as well as boys.

From the beginning of the game to the end, the action never stops. That means there isn't any of the standing around common to other sports.

It's also fun because it's a forgiving game. Drop a fly ball in baseball and you'll wish the earth would open and swallow you up. But make a mistake in soccer and hardly anyone notices.

No wonder soccer is America's hot sport. When American Sport Data asked six- to eleven-year-olds to name the sports in

From beginning to end, a soccer game can be exciting fun. The action never stops.

which they participated once a week, soccer was No. 1, more popular than softball, touch football, or baseball.

Soccer leagues are springing up in American suburbs as fast as Burger Kings. Parents sign up children as early as preschool. Adults play into middle age and beyond.

Membership in the American Youth Soccer Organization doubled to more than 700,000 over the past dozen or so years. What's interesting about the AYSO's membership statistics is that the percentage of girls has jumped from 20 percent to 40 percent. (By comparison, fewer than one-third of young basketball players are female, according to the Women's Sports Foundation.)

Much of what's happened in women's soccer has resulted from the rise in popularity of women's sports in general. Title IX, the federal law passed in 1972 that mandates that high school and college sports programs be equal for men and women, has played a role.

Then there's the women's national team. In soccer, American women are a world power.

For decades, the men's national team turned in one mediocre performance in international competition after another. When the women's team scored a stunning upset over Norway in World Cup competition in 1991, the United States had its first victory ever in international soccer.

"It's a shot in the arm for soccer in America," said Mary Harvey, the team's goalkeeper, "for men, for women, youth teams, all of us."

Even greater days soon followed. The women's team won the gold medal in the debut of women's soccer as an Olympic sport in 1996. They then captured the World Cup a second time in 1999, when the competition was held in the United States.

The worldwide success of the American women's national team provided a shot in the arm for soccer in the United States. Here the team celebrates their victory in the 1999 World Cup.

Some 650,000 tickets were sold to the 32 women's 1999 World Cup matches. More than 90,000 fans packed the Rose Bowl in Pasadena, California, for the final game. It was the biggest crowd ever to see a women's sporting event. More than 40 million Americans watched on TV.

Mia Hamm, a forward for the American team, reigned as the most popular soccer player in the country, male or female. She made commercials with Michael Jordan and had her own signature

Mia Hamm outraces Chinese opponents in 1996 Olympic competition. During the 1990s, Hamm was considered the best offensive women's soccer player in the world.

Barbie doll. By 2000, the former University of North Carolina star had scored 114 goals in international play, even more than Brazil's legendary Pelé.

The extraordinary success of the women's national team helped to make their stars into role models for girls who wanted to play soccer. More and more girls flooded into the sport.

Soccer has also exploded as a college sport. The game has certain advantages over such big-time college sports as football and basketball. To play soccer, a student can be of average size, which makes the sport accessible to more people. And soccer is an inexpensive sport to organize, a big factor to cost-conscious colleges. Today, well over a thousand four-year colleges offer soccer programs for both men and women.

The number of college soccer teams has doubled and redoubled in recent years. Yale's Hiro Suzuki (with ball) is one of the game's most dynamic players.

This book is for anyone who wants to know all there is to know about soccer. It spells out the rules (as set by the official governing body of soccer, the Fédération Internationale de Football Association, FIFA), covers playing positions and formations, and explains how to play the game. It covers professional soccer, the World Cup, and soccer as an Olympic sport. There's a glossary and a for-more-information section. As this rundown may suggest, it's a book for anyone who wants to get serious about the game.

FIFA

1

The Field and Equipment

Soccer is a simple game. Two teams of 11 players try to kick or head the ball into each other's goal. A goal counts as one point. The team that scores the most goals wins.

For young players, the official rules of the game are often bent. Having 11 players on a side is one example. Kids under 12 might play six-on-six or seven-on-seven. This gives younger players more of a chance to learn the fundamentals and have fun.

The Soccer Field

The field is a big rectangle. The official rules state that the field must be between 100 and 130 yards long and between 50 and 100 yards wide. Soccer teams in the United States frequently play on a field that is 100 yards long and 80 yards wide. This makes the soccer field only a bit shorter and about 25 yards wider than a football field (though it can be 10 yards longer and almost twice as wide).

Players between the ages of eight and twelve often use a field that is about 70 yards long and 50 yards wide, or about two-thirds

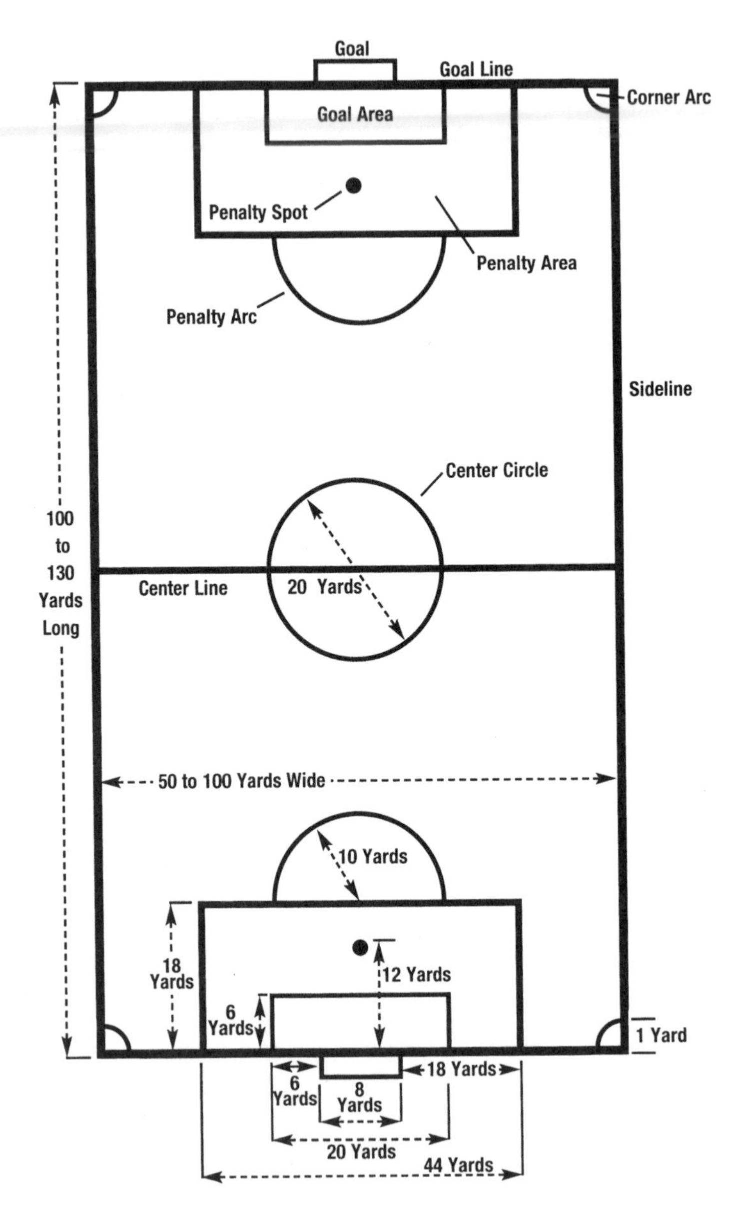

The soccer field with measurements and markings.

the size of a full-sized field. For boys and girls under the age of eight, a field that is 40 yards long and 35 yards wide is common.

At each end of the field are the goal lines, also called end lines. A goal is centered on each goal line. Each goal is eight yards wide and eight feet tall.

In front of each goal is the goal area, a rectangle that is 20 yards long and six yards deep. Enclosing the goal area is a second rectangle called the penalty area. It is 44 yards long and 18 yards deep.

A penalty spot, or mark, is centered in the penalty area at a point 12 yards from the goal. The ball is placed on the penalty spot for penalty kicks.

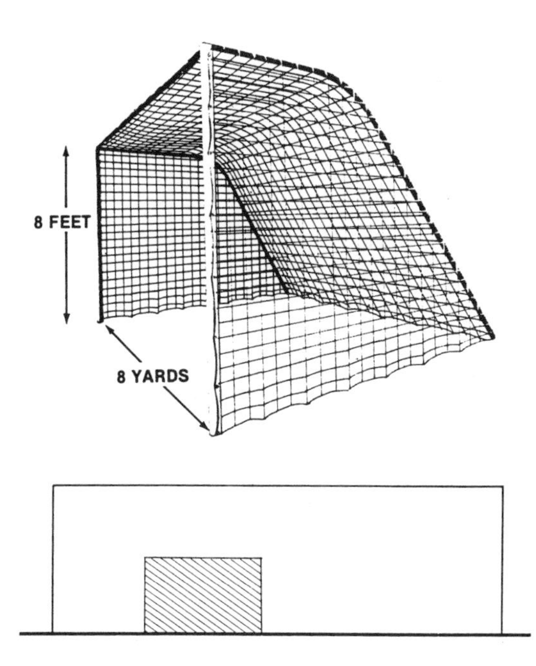

Soccer's goal is almost eight times bigger than the goal in ice hockey (shaded area).

An official game lasts 90 minutes. It is played in two 45-minute halves (not periods). For young players, games are shorter. Boys and girls from 14 to 16 often play 40-minute halves. For younger players, games with 35- or 30-minute halves are common.

In some leagues, teams play a 10-minute or 15-minute sudden-death overtime period if the score is tied at the end of regulation play. The first team to score wins. More than one overtime period may be needed if the score remains tied after the first extra period.

A tie game can also be decided by penalty kicks. Each team gets five penalty kicks at the opposition goal. The team that scores the most goals out of the five tries is declared the winner. In 1999, the Women's World Cup was decided in this manner, with the U.S. team winning on Brandi Chastain's penalty kick after a scoreless tie.

A referee supervises play. He or she serves as the game's time-keeper and is responsible for the conduct of the game and for penalizing players who break the rules or commit fouls.

One or two linesmen often assist the referee. The linesmen patrol the sidelines, indicating when and where the ball has gone out of bounds.

Equipment

You can play soccer just about anywhere. Once you establish the size of the playing field, you can use jackets or backpacks to mark the goals. But when it comes to the ball, you can't improvise. It's not soccer without the real thing.

A regulation ball is made of black and white leather, is 27 to 28

The ball is constructed of 32 black and white panels. (Twelve are five-sided; 20 are six-sided.) Panels make it easier to tell exactly how a fast-moving ball is spinning.

inches in circumference, and weighs between 14 and 16 ounces. It is known as a size 5 ball.

Players from eight to twelve years old normally use a smaller ball, a size 4, that is between 25 and 26 inches in circumference and weighs from 11 to 13 ounces.

For still younger players, there is a size 3 ball, which is 24 to 25 inches in circumference.

Soccer shoes are studded with hard rubber cleats.

Clothing

When it comes to clothing, you need soccer shoes, or cleats, as they are called. You need shin guards, a jersey, shorts, and socks.

• **CLEATS**—The right shoes are vital. Take your time making your selection.

In 1999 Nike introduced cleats especially for girls and women. Called the Air Zoom M9, in honor of Mia Hamm, one of the stars of the U.S. World Cup team, the shoe has a more arched heel and is tapered to fit a woman's narrow foot.

Take care of your shoes. If they get wet during a game or practice session, allow them to dry slowly. Stuffing them with newspaper aids the drying process and helps the shoes to keep their shape.

• **SOCKS**—Soccer socks are extra long, stretching all the way to the knee. The top is folded down to form an inverted cuff.

• **SHIN GUARDS**—Curved and molded lengths of plastic, your shin guards slide into your socks and are held in place by them. You might prefer, however, the type of shin guard that attaches to your leg with a Velcro strap.

You're sure to find that you can run faster without shin guards, but don't even think of discarding them. Shin guards are needed to prevent bruises and even fractures.

• **JERSEYS**—Loose-fitting jerseys can be short-sleeved or long-sleeved. Long sleeves are for cold weather.

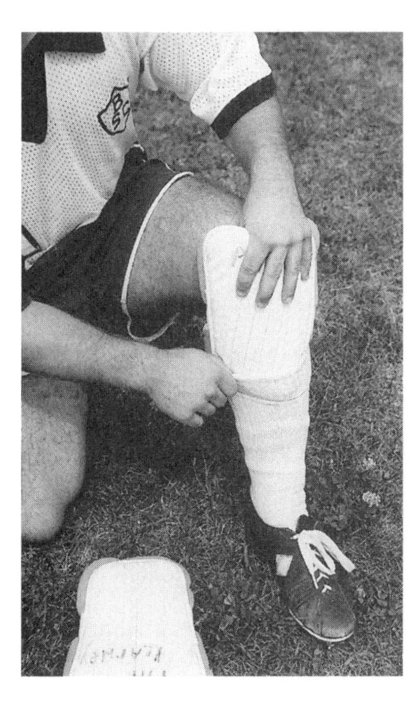

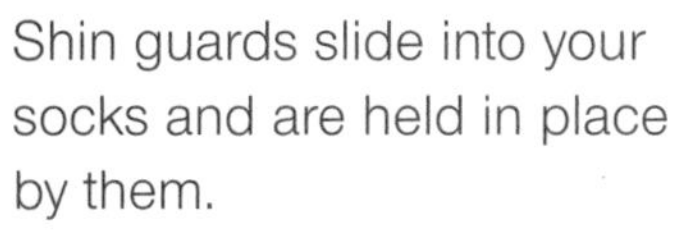

Shin guards slide into your socks and are held in place by them.

Jerseys should be loose fitting so you can move your arms freely.

• **SHORTS**—Most soccer shorts are loose-fitting, too. You want to be able to move freely.

Clothing for goalies is somewhat different. The color of the goalie's shirt contrasts sharply with the shirts of his teammates. Indeed, some goalies' shirts feature vivid colors and wild patterns.

Shirts for goalies are usually long-sleeved with padding at the elbows. There are also special shorts for goalies. They're a bit longer than the shorts worn by other players, and they're padded at the sides.

Most goalies wear gloves. There are a number of different types, but all are designed to improve the goalie's ability to catch and grip the ball.

During a game or practice session, don't wear anything that could be dangerous. Necklaces, rings, earrings, or watches can catch on another player. Soccer is a relatively safe sport, but wearing needless jewelry increases the risk of injury.

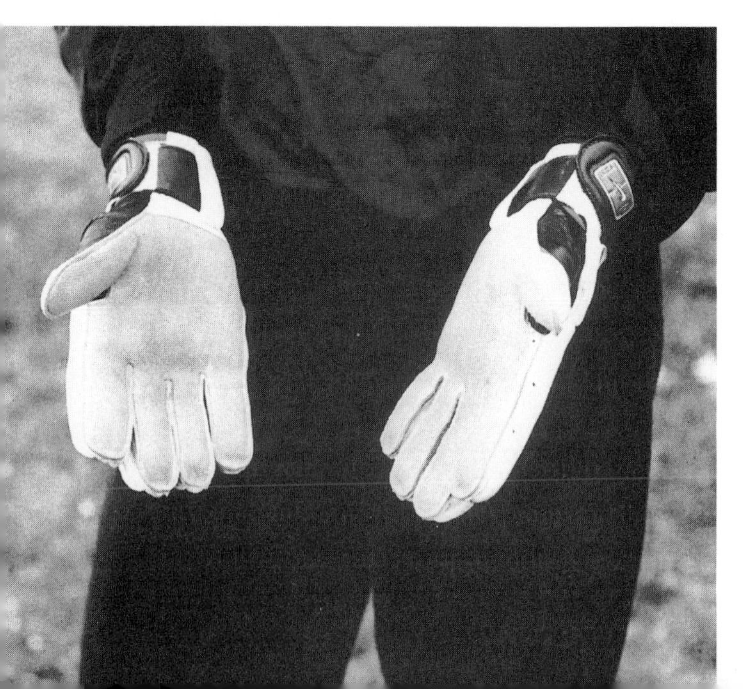

Goalkeepers often wear gloves like these.

The Players

According to the official rules of soccer, there are two positions on the 11-person soccer team: one goalkeeper and ten field players. Soccer teams go beyond the official rules by organizing the field players into three distinct groups: forwards, midfielders, and defenders.

While each of these has basic tasks to perform, the positions are not fixed as to what portion of the field each must occupy. Soccer is a free-flowing game. Once the action begins, a forward, normally an attacking player, can be called upon to defend. A defender can go on the attack.

At the same time, certain duties and responsibilities go with each position. The pages that follow explain them.

Forwards

A forward's job is to score. Most teams have two or three forwards, but the number can be as low as one or as high as five.

As a forward, you have to be fast. You have to have the ability to outrun the opposition's defensive players.

You also have to be exceptionally skilled in soccer's basics. You have to be a clever dribbler to outmaneuver the defense. You have to be sure and confident in heading the ball, for often you'll be called upon to head high balls that are passed in from the sideline or that result from corner kicks.

At Saint Louis University, forward Matt McKeon (left) shattered collegiate scoring records.

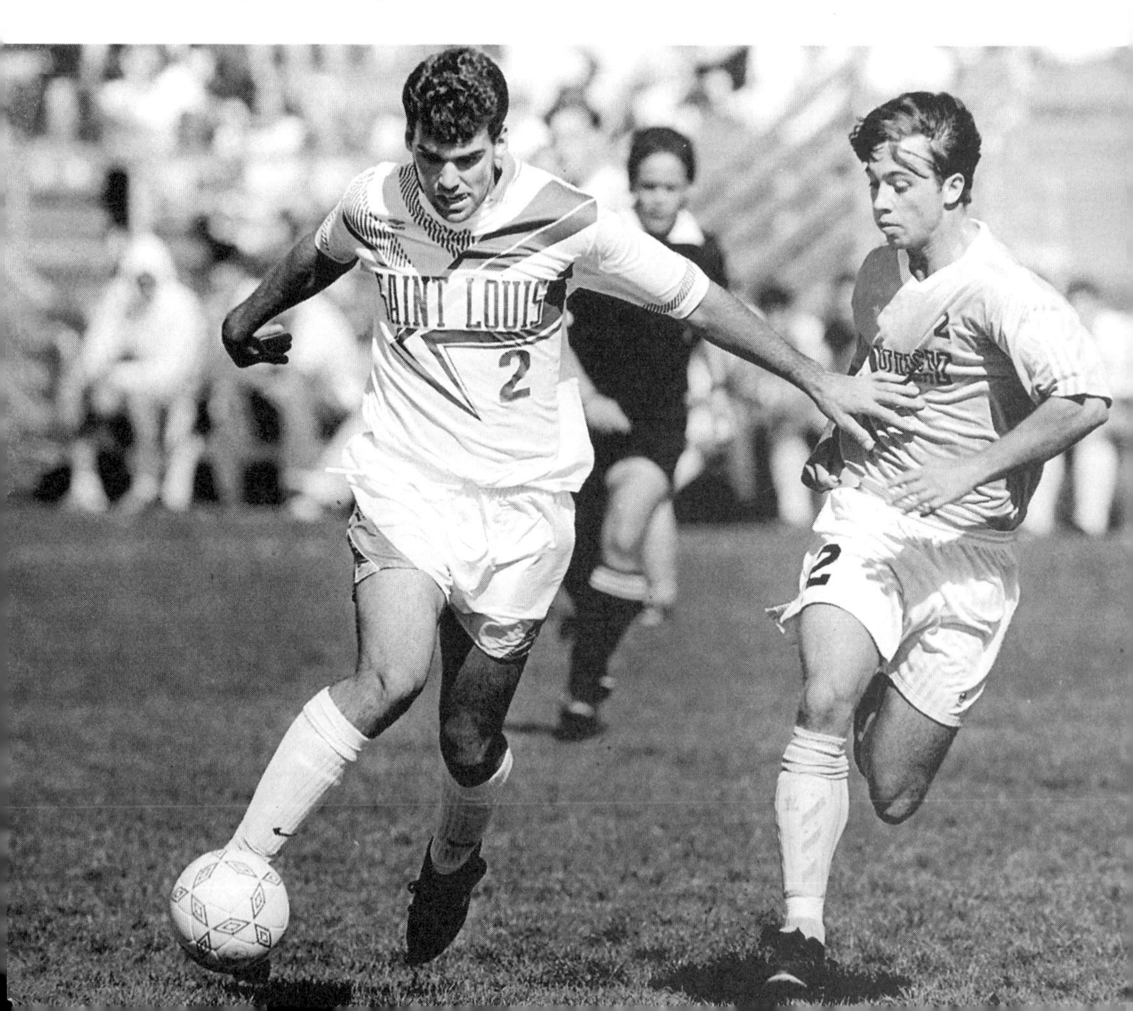

Forward Diego Serna is a featured performer for Major League Soccer's Miami Fusion.

Since the forwards are the team's scorers, you have to be skilled in the different ways of shooting the ball. You don't have to be an outstanding passer to be a forward. You don't have to feel that you have to share the ball with anyone. Putting the ball into the net is what your coach and teammates want you to be able to do.

Midfielders have to be in great shape because they're constantly running from one end of the field to the other.

Midfielders

Some coaches make their best players midfielders. Since they're stationed at midfield, between the forwards and defenders, midfielders have to use both offensive and defensive skills.

As is the case with forwards, the number of midfielders on a team can vary. Most teams play with three, four, or five midfielders. But the number can be as few as two or as many as six.

As a midfielder, you have to be particularly adept at passing. You have to be able to pass forward, back, and from one side of the field to the other. And because you're going to spend the game running up and down virtually the entire length of the field, you have to have great stamina.

Midfielders often get as close to the goal as the forwards do, so they have to have the ability to bang the ball into the net. Midfielders also have a wide range of defensive responsibilities. When the ball is at the other end of the field, the midfielders are expected to defend the goal and mark a particular player.

Coaches want midfielders who have good leadership qualities. They look for players who have the ability to communicate well with their teammates in helping to blend the team's offense and defense.

Defenders

Defensive players, often called fullbacks, are responsible for stopping any opposition attack. Most teams have three or four defenders, but once in a while a team will field formations that call for only two defensive backs or as many as five of them.

As a defender, you'll be expected to steal the ball and intercept passes. This takes good speed and determination. It also takes a willingness to want to play an opponent as well as the ball. You have to be able to endure a good measure of bone-jarring collisions with other players. It helps to be aggressive and have a strong body when you're a defensive back.

Defensive players often move forward together in a line. A fullback that remains too far back can create a problem for the team. Opposition forwards can then operate close to the goal since they have less fear of drawing an offside call. (The offside rule states that a player without the ball must keep two defensive players between him- or herself and the opposing team's goal.)

Defensive players must be skilled at intercepting and stealing the ball.

Defenders can also have offensive responsibilities and have to keep alert for the chance to launch an offensive thrust. This opportunity often comes when clearing the ball from in front of the goal.

No matter what position you play, your duties and responsibilities can vary from minute to minute during a game. The score of the game, the team's overall strategy, your opponent's strategy, where the ball happens to be on the field—all of these have a bearing on what you should be doing at any given moment.

Never forget that soccer is a team game. This means that you should be aware of where each of your teammates is positioned and where each is going to be positioned. With this understanding you'll be better able to move with the ball and pass it in a way that will do your team the most good.

Goalkeeping

As a goalkeeper, you're the last line of defense. It's a difficult and demanding job—one that requires agility and outstanding ball-handling skills, plus intelligence and good judgment.

Soccer is a low-scoring game. A single goal sometimes decides matters. Thus, the goalie usually ends up the hero or the goat. Being a goat can be very unpleasant. Take the case of Brazil's Moaeyr Barbosa. For years he reigned as one of his nation's all-time great goalkeepers. Then Barbosa failed to block the winning goal in Uruguay's shocking victory over Brazil in the 1950 World Cup.

For the rest of his life, Barbosa was made to feel disgraced. In 1994, 44 years after the incident, the coach of the Brazilian World Cup team asked Barbosa not to pose for a photograph with the players because he might bring the team bad luck.

To be a goalkeeper, you have to have several specialized skills. These include quick reflexes, good hands, and the ability to kick the ball a long distance (much the way a punter does in football). And, as the Barbosa incident suggests, you have to be resilient.

It's not easy being a goalkeeper. You have to be both bold and fearless.

The rules recognize the goalkeeper as being special. You're the only player permitted to use your hands when playing the ball. And since you play with your back to the goal, you're the only player on your team with a view of the whole field.

Some goalies have the ability to make the job look easy. They're always in the right position. The ball seems to be magically drawn to their hands. Other goalkeepers are constantly leaping and diving to make saves. They're soccer acrobats.

The difference is often in concentration. The goalkeeper that seems not to have to move for the ball keeps focused on the game at all times. He or she is able to realize in advance where the shot is going to be coming from, and adjust his or her body position accordingly. Having this positional sense is one of the basics of successful goaltending.

Goalkeepers have to be aggressive, too, ready to dash out of the goal toward the ball. This is Bill May, goalkeeper of the University of Washington Huskies.

As a goalkeeper, take your stance in the center of the goal, three or four feet in front of the goal line. Bend your knees slightly. Keep alert. Move from one side to the other as the ball moves. When the ball is being played on the right side of the field, for instance, move to that side, keeping yourself positioned between the ball and the goal. Hold your hands at about chest level. Be ready to spring for the ball.

Sometimes your strategy should be to play aggressively, to move out of the goal toward the ball. In so doing, you cut the shooter's target area.

Playing aggressively can produce other benefits. When you move toward the ball and the shooter, you may cause the player to panic and shoot too quickly. You can get an easy save as a result.

Since you're closer to the ball after leaving the goal, there may be a chance for you to snatch it away. This is especially true if the potential shooter allows the ball to get too far out in front of his or her feet.

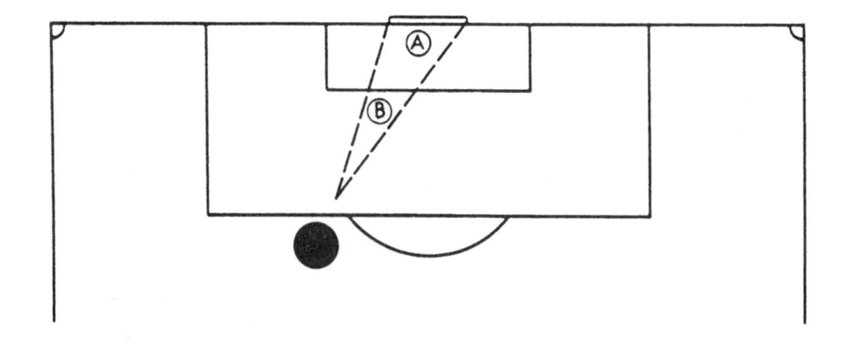

By leaving the goal and advancing toward the attacking player (from position A to position B), the goalkeeper trims down the target area.

Each of the various types of shots you face as a goalie requires different catching skills. But no matter the kind of shot that comes toward you, the most important rule in making a save is to get your body behind the ball. Then, if you don't make the catch cleanly or you bobble the ball, it's less likely to end up in the net. The chances are that it will fall at your feet and you can smother it.

- **LOW SHOTS**—On low shots, those that cling to the ground, get down on one knee in front of the ball and scoop it up with both hands. Field the ball in somewhat the same way a baseball outfielder handles a ground ball, blocking it with your body.

Always position yourself behind the ball. Grab it with both hands; hug it to your chest.

Never take your eyes off the ball. Watch it until you have it in your hands. Follow this rule every time you move to make a catch.

- **MID-LEVEL SHOTS**—When the ball comes toward you at about belt level, again get in front of it. Keep your elbows close to your body. Pull the ball toward your midsection, letting your hands and belly absorb the ball's impact. On such shots, remember that you don't have to wait for the ball to come to you; you can leave the goal and meet it.

- **HIGH SHOTS**—On high shots that are catchable, get your hands high above your head, the fingers spread, the thumbs almost touching. When your hands are correctly positioned, your thumbs and forefingers together form the letter W. The hands should be in back of the ball as you make the catch.

When the ball is driven high above your upstretched hands and there's no chance to make the catch, leap into the air and deflect the ball over the crossbar. Some goalies use a fist to do this. Others use their fingertips.

While most people look upon the goalie as a defensive player, there are times you play an important role on offense. As soon as you get control of the ball, get it back in play fast. In throwing the ball, you're allowed to take four running steps before releasing it. Take more than four steps and the opposition gets awarded an indirect free kick.

Throw with one hand. Throw hard and keep the ball low. You don't want to risk an interception.

If a teammate is close by and not being guarded, pass the ball by rolling it. By putting the ball at your teammate's feet, he or she will then be able to quickly pass or dribble.

On high shots, you can use your fist to deflect the ball over the crossbar.

If you can't find a teammate to pass to, you'll have to kick the ball away. You can use a drop kick or you can punt the ball.

• **THE DROP KICK**—For a drop kick, simply hold the ball in front of your body, let it fall to the ground in front of your feet, and kick it as it rebounds. While the drop kick makes it easy to get the ball away quickly, it takes perfect timing, and so is often difficult for young players.

• **PUNTING**—Punting is easier. In punting, use a three-step approach. Holding the ball out in front of your body, step with your right foot, then your left, then boot the ball away (use the opposite order if you are a lefty). Make contact with your instep and follow through. Your kicking foot should finish at about the level of your head. A good punt will travel 40 or 50 yards, almost to the field's center line.

When you punt, try to target a teammate. But getting the ball to a teammate is no easy task. With most punts, the ball is in the air so long that the players on the opposition team have the time to get downfield and cover the intended receiver. In addition, when the ball does come down, it plummets so fast that it's difficult to control. If the teammate you picked out ends up with the ball, consider it good luck more than anything else.

Besides knowing what to do during the normal flow of a game, the goalkeeper has to be prepared to cope with several special challenges. These include:

• **CORNER KICK**—When the opposition is awarded a corner kick, it puts extra pressure on the goalkeeper. The kicker is going to try to execute a crossing pass, sending the ball parallel to the goal

When no teammate is open, punting is often the goalkeeper's only option. It's the best way to get the ball far away from the goal.

line a few feet above the ground, so a forward can try to head the ball into the net.

In defending against a corner kick, take a stance close to the goalpost that's farthest from the kicker. As the ball is kicked, start forward and grab the ball before the opponent can head it.

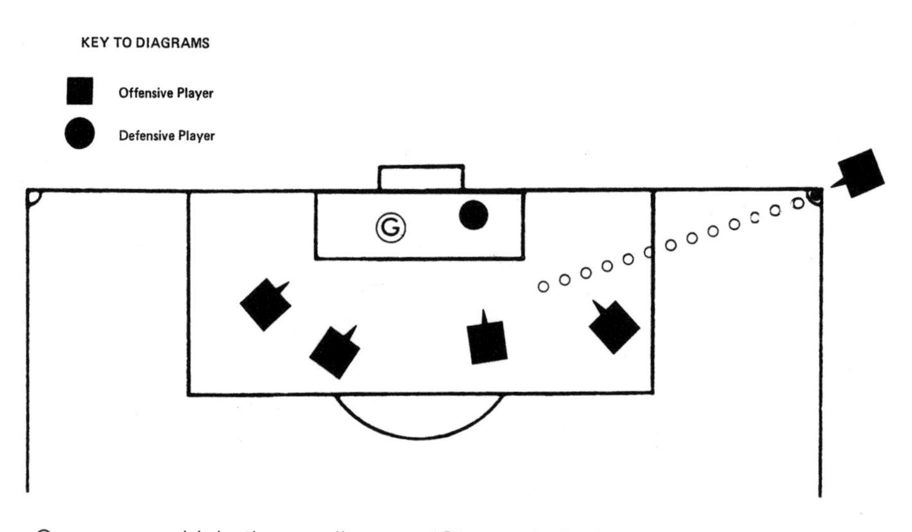

On a corner kick, the goalkeeper (G) gets help from a teammate who is positioned near the post closest to the kicker.

- **DIRECT AND INDIRECT FREE KICKS**—When the opposition is awarded a direct or indirect free kick in front of the goal, special defensive strategy is required. Set up a line—a wall—of four players between the goal and the ball to block the ball. The first player in the line should stand between the goalpost nearest the ball and the ball itself. As the goalie, you should position yourself in front of the goal, covering the open area near the far post. (Free kicks are also discussed in Chapter 8.)

• **PENALTY KICK**—The penalty kick is the goalie's toughest challenge. The advantage is with the kicker.

About all that you can do in defending against a penalty kick is decide in advance which side of the goal the kicker is going to be aiming for. As soon as the kicker's foot touches the ball, dive for that side. If you guessed right, you might make the save. If you were wrong, don't worry about it.

Keep in mind that the goalie also has a leadership role to play during a game. This is especially true in the penalty area, which you should look upon as your own domain. Take control when play moves into the penalty area. When you dash out of the goal to make

Courageous Briana Scurry, goalkeeper for the U.S. women's national team.

a save, shout "Goalie! Goalie!" This will signal your teammates to step aside and allow you to play the ball.

Since you have a better view of the playing field than anyone else does, you can tell your teammates which opponents to cover. When you have to vacate the goal to get the ball, instruct a teammate to take over for you.

You can't do everything. You need help. During the Women's World Cup final, midfielder Kristine Lilly robbed China of a victory in overtime by heading the ball out of the goal.

Before you decide to become a goalkeeper, give the matter serious thought. You have to be able to face shots traveling at bullet speed. You have to be willing to leap headlong for shots to your right or left. You have to be able to dive headfirst at the feet of an onrushing shooter. Along with the many skills that the position requires, being a goalkeeper takes a large amount of courage.

The Rules

A video titled *Soccer's Hard Men* was released in Great Britain several years ago. It recalled the dirty tactics of Britain's most notorious soccer toughs. Such players as Ron "Chopper" Harris and Norman "Bites Yer Legs" Hunter were shown fouling opponents with a poke in the eye or an elbow behind the ear. Trampling on an opponent's toes was another technique they used.

Soccer's rules, like those of other team sports, seek to prevent such conduct and explain what to do as well as what not to do. This section examines the most important of them.

The Coin Toss

A soccer game begins with a coin toss. The winner of the coin toss kicks off.

It used to be that the team winning the toss was able to choose either to kick off or choose a particular goal it wanted to defend. Not anymore. In 1998, the rule was changed. Now the winner of the toss *must* kick off.

The team losing the coin toss gets to pick which end of the field it wants to defend. In deciding, consider wind conditions and the position of the sun. Ideally, you want both the wind and the sun to be at your back. (After halftime, teams switch goals. The team that did not kick off at the beginning of the game kicks off at the start of the second half.)

The Kickoff

For the kickoff the ball is placed in the center of the field. All players must remain in their half of the field until the ball is put in play, with defensive players at least 10 yards from the ball.

On a signal from the referee, the ball is kicked into the opponent's end of the field. Usually the kicker simply taps the ball to a teammate, but sometimes he or she will slam the ball deep into opposition territory. The kicker is not permitted to play the ball a second time until it is played by an opposition player.

A kickoff is also used to put the ball in play after a goal has been scored. The team that was scored upon receives the kickoff.

After the kickoff, the ball remains in play with players moving it up and down the field unless it crosses a goal line or a sideline, or a player commits a foul. There are no time-outs in soccer.

In moving the ball, you can use any part of your body except your hands and arms. The goalkeeper is the only player permitted to touch the ball with his or her hands or arms.

Restarts

If the ball goes out of bounds, the referee's whistle sounds and play is halted. The game is restarted with a throw-in, a goal kick, or a corner kick.

• **THROW-IN**—When the ball goes out of bounds over a sideline, it's put back in play with a throw-in. As in basketball, if the ball was last touched by team A, team B takes the throw-in. This is the only time a player other than the goalkeeper is allowed to use his or her hands.

In executing a throw-in, both hands must be used and the ball must be thrown from behind and over the head. Both feet must be on the ground when the ball leaves the player's hands.

On a throw-in, get your hands behind the ball.

• **CORNER KICK**—When a member of the defending team causes the ball to go over the goal line, play is restarted with a corner kick made by a member of the offensive team. The ball is placed within the corner arc on the side of the goal from which it went out of bounds. Members of the other team must stay at least 10 yards from the ball until it is in play.

• **GOAL KICK**—If a member of the attacking team causes the ball to go over the goal line, it is put back in play with a goal kick taken by a member of the defensive team.

The kick is taken from anywhere inside the goal area. Most players, however, place the ball in a corner of the goal area, so the ball is as far away from the goal as possible.

As the kick is being taken, members of the attacking team must stay outside the penalty area. The ball must clear the penalty area before another player is permitted to touch it.

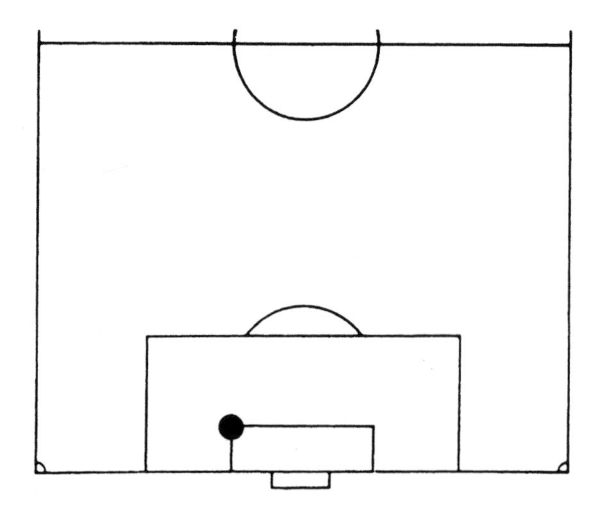

For a goal kick, the ball is placed in a corner of the goal area.

• **THE DROP KICK**—Suppose a stray dog runs out onto the field and interferes with play. In this and other unusual circumstances, the referee is likely to halt the game and call for a drop kick.

The drop kick is similar to ice hockey's faceoff. The referee drops the ball between two opposing players who have been chosen by their coaches. They attempt to pass or gain control of the ball the instant that it hits the ground.

Fouls

As in other team sports, the rules of soccer make an effort to maintain law and order. For any violation of the rules, a penalty is called against the guilty individual or his or her team. Most soccer fouls are punished by a free kick of one type or another.

• **INDIRECT FREE KICK**—When a player is guilty of dangerous play, an indirect free kick is called. Indirect-kick fouls include:

OBSTRUCTING an opponent
CHARGING the goalkeeper
INTERFERENCE by the goalkeeper
TIME-WASTING by the goalkeeper
AN OFFSIDE violation (see below)

Opposing players must remain at least 10 yards from the ball as it is being kicked. A goal cannot be scored directly from an indirect free kick; that is, the ball must be touched by at least one other player before entering the goal.

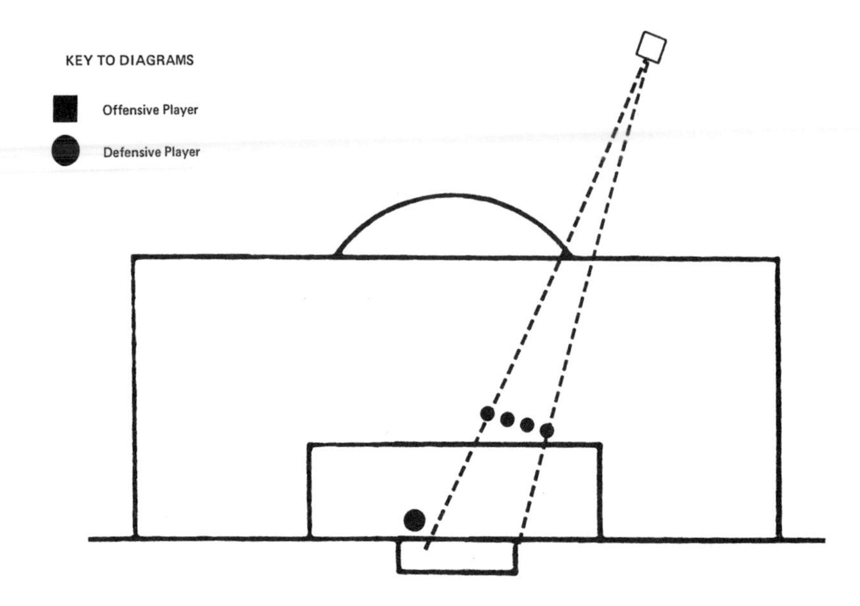

Defensive players construct a wall to protect the goal from indirect free kicks and direct free kicks. Once the wall is set, the goalkeeper protects the open space that remains.

- **DIRECT FREE KICK**—When a player commits a serious offense against an opponent, a direct free kick is called. Offenses that result in this penalty include:

KICKING or attempting to kick an opponent
PUSHING an opponent
TRIPPING an opponent
JUMPING into or running into an opponent
CHARGING an opponent in a violent manner
HITTING or attempting to hit an opponent

HOLDING an opponent with one's hand or arm
TACKLING an opponent rather than the ball
A HANDBALL (playing the ball with any part of
the hands or arms)

A direct kick is taken from the point where the foul took place. Players on the defending team must keep at least 10 yards from the ball as it is being kicked, as in an indirect free kick. It's called a *direct* free kick because a goal may be scored directly from the kick; no other player has to touch it.

- **PENALTY KICK**—When a player commits a direct-kick foul within the penalty box, serious punishment results. The opposition is awarded a penalty kick.

The ball is placed on the penalty spot and a player is assigned to take a shot against the opposition goalie. No other players are permitted within the penalty box. It's a tense duel between the kicker and the goalie, and the kicker usually wins.

Offside Rule

In the early days of soccer, a common piece of strategy called for teams to station one or two players close to the opposition goal. When the team got possession, the ball would immediately be passed to one of the two "sleepers," as they were often called. A goal would frequently result. Soccer's offside rule is meant to prevent such "goal hanging" and the easy scores that it permits.

A violation of the offside rule occurs when an attacking player,

KEY TO DIAGRAMS

■ Offensive Player

● Defensive Player

The offensive player closest to the goal is offside here. That's because there is only one defensive player (the goalkeeper) and no ball between that player and the goal.

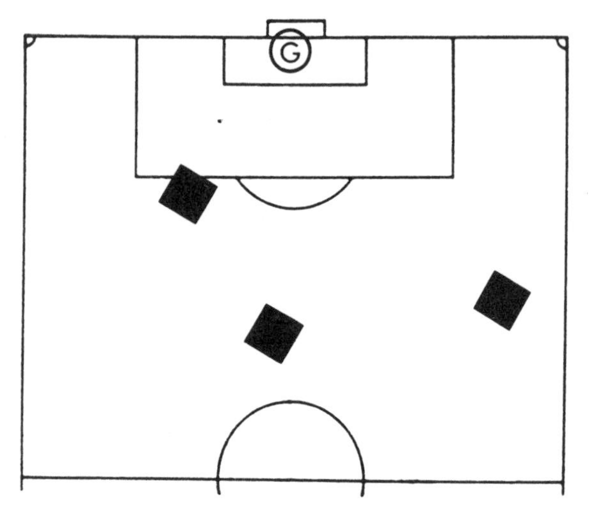

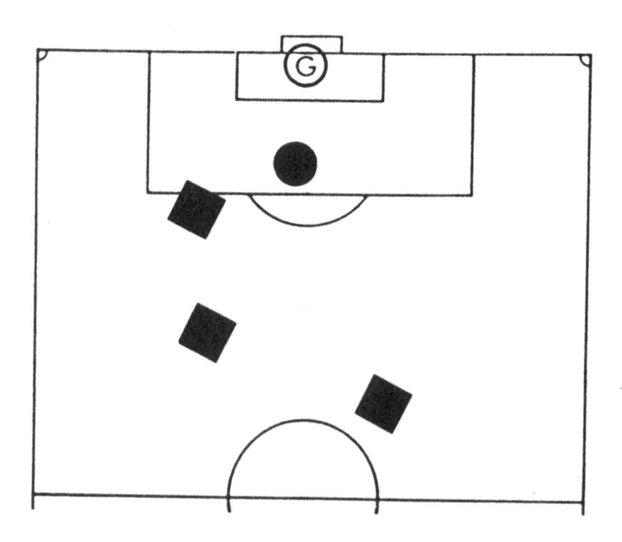

There is no off-side violation in this diagram, since a second defensive player is now positioned between the offensive player and the goal.

without the ball, fails to keep two players between himself or herself and the opposition goal.

The rule is not as severe as it sounds. First of all, the goalie is one of the two players to which the rule refers. Second, the rule can be applied only when you're in the attacking half of the field.

What the offside rule boils down to is this: When you don't have the ball, keep one opposing player plus the goalie between yourself and their goal. Break the rule, and your team will be penalized with an indirect free kick.

Other Rule Violations

Normally, when a player violates one of soccer's rules, the referee blows the whistle, the game is halted, a direct or indirect kick is taken, and then play resumes. But when a player is guilty of a very serious foul, or commits one foul after another, more serious action may be taken.

The referee has two plastic cards in his shirt pocket, each about the size of a playing card. One card is yellow, the other red.

The yellow card is a warning card. If a player persists in disobeying the rules, argues with the referee, or is guilty of unsportsmanlike conduct, the referee holds up the yellow card for the guilty player, other officials, and other players to see.

It's a signal that the player is being cautioned. If the player continues to be a problem, serious punishment could follow. In addition, the referee awards an indirect free kick to the opposing team each time the yellow card is shown.

The red card is given to a player for any flagrant foul, such as blocking a player who has a scoring opportunity. It's also given for the use of bad language or for repeated yellow-card offenses. When a player is given a red card, it's a signal that he or she is being sent off the field. The team is not permitted to use a replacement. They must play the rest of the game with 10 players, a serious handicap.

Soccer Skills

Kicking, dribbling, and heading are the basic soccer skills you have to have. They're vital to passing, shooting, and defending.

Mastering these skills takes time. Be prepared for plenty of practice sessions. Even world-class players constantly practice the basic skills.

But another skill you can't overlook is running. In soccer, you're seldom still. Sometimes you're running at three-quarters speed, sometimes you're sprinting. You're always on the move. In the average soccer game, players spend about 75 percent of their time running.

Keep relaxed when you run. Keep your head and shoulders back. Don't bend forward.

Your arms should help you in moving forward. Keep your elbows close to your body. Pump your arms back and forth.

As you stride, point each foot straight ahead. Reach out with your toes to make each stride as long as possible.

Keep your head and shoulders back when you run. You hands and arms should pump forward. Stride ahead on your toes. This is UCLA's Skylar Little.

When each heel lands, roll forward onto your toes so you can push off on the next stride. Avoid landing flat-footed.

Never try running fast until you're warmed up. This is especially true on cold days. Spend at least 10 or 15 minutes getting loose. Do some light jogging. Otherwise, you run the risk of muscle injury.

Kicking

There was only the tiniest space between the goalkeeper and the left post. From 19 yards out, Shannon MacMillan of the American team ripped a shot toward the slim opening. The ball rocketed toward the net. The North Korean goalkeeper dived, thrusting out her hands. But she ended up with only fistfuls of air.

The Americans downed the Koreans, 3–0, in their quarterfinal match-up during the World Cup competition in 1999. Forward MacMillan, 24 years old, a native of Syosset, New York, who grew up in Escondido, California, was an important factor. Besides the goal she scored, she assisted on the other two.

A four-time All-American at the University of Portland, MacMillan kicked with tremendous power. "The ball moves around," said Briana Scurry, one of MacMillan's teammates. "It knuckles and dips. She hits it harder than anyone else on the team."

Kicking is soccer's basic skill. You want to be able to kick hard (hard enough to burn a goalie), and you want to be able to kick accurately. Hard kicks won't mean much unless you're able to pinpoint where they're going.

In most cases, you'll want to kick the ball so that it travels just above ground level. The key to executing a grass-cutter is to plant your nonkicking foot next to the ball—not behind it—as you move to kick. Keep your head down, your eyes on the ball.

Then swing the kicking leg forward, with the toes pointed downward. Kick the ball with your instep, the bony part of the foot in front of the ankle. "Kick it in the shoelaces," your coach may say to you.

Follow through by swinging your foot "through" the ball after you make contact.

You should also learn to kick the ball with both the inside and outside of the foot. Suppose you're racing downfield, dribbling the ball as you go. An opponent moves up to tackle you. Before the tackler arrives, you can use the side of your foot to quickly flick the ball to a teammate.

Or maybe your strategy should be a heel pass. Using your heel, punch the ball backward to a teammate.

There are several other kinds of kicks you'll want to learn. To loft the ball high into the air, make contact with your instep below the center of the ball, almost underneath it. Lean backward slightly as you kick. Remember to keep your eyes on the ball as your foot makes contact.

The chip is also a lofted kick, but it travels only a short distance. Again, get your foot underneath the ball, and scoop the ball into the air.

Whether you are naturally right-footed or left-footed, to become a good soccer player, you must become skilled in kicking the ball with both feet. This takes practice. If you're right-footed, kicking with your left foot is going to be difficult at first. But keep practicing. In time, you'll overcome the awkward feeling.

Point your non-kicking foot in the direction that you want the ball to go; keep your head down; follow through.

Dribbling

Dribbling is moving with the ball, in control, at your feet. Advanced players make dribbling look effortless. Their opponents make futile efforts to get the ball. Spectators look on in awe. At top levels, dribbling can be magical.

From day one on the soccer field, every player can dribble. At the beginning, players prefer to dribble mostly with one foot, their dominant kicking foot, and even with just one part of that foot.

You have to learn to use both feet when dribbling, and you must use every part of each foot—the inside and the outside, the toe and instep, the sole and heel.

Begin practicing by merely walking forward with the ball at your feet. Tap it with the inside of one foot, then the inside of the other. Simply nudge the ball forward. Don't attempt to kick it. The ball should never be more than a foot or so in front of your feet.

Gradually increase your pace until you're dribbling at a slow jog. Tap the ball forward on every step. As you keep increasing your speed, try tapping the ball on every other step. But don't let the ball get more than two or three feet ahead of you. Use the outside of each foot as well as the inside. Use your toes and insteps.

A good way to develop the ball-handling skills important to dribbling is with a drill called juggling. In this, you keep the ball continuously in the air without using your hands or arms.

Begin by dropping the ball from your hands to the top of your thigh, and then pop it upward. Using your feet, head, and thighs, keep bouncing the ball back up in the air. At first, you may be able to execute only two or three rebounds. But keep trying to stretch the number.

Juggling the ball—keeping it in the air without using your hands or arms—will help you to develop ball-handling skills.

Keep your eyes on the ball when you move to head it.
Ashlee Richmond of the University of Oklahoma demonstrates.

Heading

Once you're playing soccer, there is going to come a time when, on a corner kick or crossing pass, the ball is going to be booted across the field and end up five or six feet above the ground right in front of the goal. And you're going to be there.

You can't trap the ball and drop it at your feet. Opposition players will pounce on it.

What you have to be able to do is spring into the air and make contact with your forehead, banging the ball toward the net. You have to head the ball. Heading is as basic to soccer as running and cleated shoes.

You use your forehead to head the ball. Keep your eyes open as the ball comes toward you. It's natural to want to shut your eyes, but you have to learn to overcome this tendency.

You also want to attack the ball. What you must not do is calmly wait for the ball to strike your forehead. Just before the ball makes contact, lunge for it, getting power from your upper body, not your legs.

If you've never tried heading, begin with these drills: Simply touch the ball to your forehead, keeping your eyes open. Then toss the ball up a short distance, a foot or so, and head it. Catch the ball. Toss it up again and head it again. Do it over and over.

Once you feel confident, and you're sure you're keeping your eyes open, try heading the ball a second time instead of catching it.

Another exercise is to pair off with a teammate. Sit facing one another. Your toes should be touching. Your knees should be bent. Have your partner gently toss the ball toward your forehead. Head it back. Remember, don't wait for it to arrive. Tilt your head back as the ball drops toward you, then snap your head forward to make contact.

After several tosses, reverse roles. You toss; your partner heads.

As you repeat the drill, keep moving farther apart. Once you and your partner feel skilled, switch to a kneeling position. Then try standing and heading.

During a game, you'll seldom be able to head the ball from a standing position. In almost every case, you'll have to spring into the air to make contact.

Leaping and heading is much like rebounding in basketball. Proper timing is the key factor. You have to time your jump so that you're reaching maximum height as the ball arrives. Most young players jump too late. The ball whizzes by and they never touch it.

Heading is not fundamentally dangerous. But the best way to avoid getting hurt is to head the ball properly. This means watching the ball carefully and being aggressive as you move to make contact.

Practice with a teammate. Have the teammate toss the ball so that it arrives about a foot or so above the level of your head. Jump up and head it back. Keep repeating the drill. Good timing comes from practice.

On the Attack

If you've ever watched World Cup soccer competition on TV, you've seen the scorer's explosions of joy whenever a ball is slammed into the net. Sometimes the scorer drops to both knees, looks toward the heavens, and clasps both hands in front of his or her chest, as if giving thanks. Then there's the scorer who turns and sprints wildly back up the field, often with both arms outstretched. And don't forget Brandi Chastain. After her game-winning kick in the 1999 Women's World Cup final, she whipped off her jersey and twirled it over her head as the huge crowd roared.

Such displays are easy to understand. Putting the ball into the net is the object of the game. A spirited display is to be expected.

While the scorer is always the hero of the moment, the truth is that most goals are the result of teamwork. Working together, players build up an attack that opens up the defense to create space for a forward to make the final strike.

Good passing is vital to such tactical maneuvering. Indeed, soccer is a passing game. Every player has to have the ability to get the ball to a teammate who is in a better position to advance or shoot.

Passing

All of your soccer skills are involved in passing. When passing, you can use either foot, either shoulder, or your head. Your passes can be hard or soft, long or short, or high or low.

For short passes, use the inside or outside of your foot. Think of your foot as being like a putter in golf. The golfer uses a putter to sweep the ball toward the hole, being careful to follow through on each stroke.

When you pass, sweep your foot into the ball. This passer is midfielder Simon Neery of Indiana University.

The heel pass looks like this.

Don't stop your foot on impact; follow through.

That's what you must do when you pass the ball—follow through. After you make contact, your foot must follow in the direction of the pass.

Also use the outside of your foot to pass.

Every time you pass, you have to consider both the direction and the pace of the ball, and your intended receiver. You want to lead your teammate with the ball, that is, pass to where the teammate is going to be.

Pace is just as important as being accurate. If the pass is too slow, the ball can be intercepted. If it's a hard pass, your teammate may not be able to control it.

If you're dribbling before you make the pass, you'll have the ball at your feet and under control. It should be easy for you to get the ball away. But if you're on the receiving end of a pass from a teammate, you must be able to stop the ball and get it under control before you attempt to pass.

Often you can use the inside of one foot or the other to stop the ball. Your foot must "give" slightly as the ball arrives. Otherwise, the ball can rebound away. Or pluck the ball out of the air with the inside of your lower leg or thigh and let it drop at your feet.

You can also use your chest to trap the ball. After impact, simply let the ball drop to your feet.

Practice passing and receiving passes with a teammate. As you move downfield together, several yards apart, pass the ball back and forth. As you run, gradually increase the distance of your passes.

Trap the ball with your chest, then let it drop to your feet.

Shooting

If you become skilled at passing, you'll be a good scorer, too. After all, a scoring shot is simply a pass that travels beyond the goalie's reach.

There are several different ways to shoot the ball. The power shot is used the most. You simply use your instep to drive the ball as hard as you can.

Sometimes a bullet isn't necessary. Suppose the ball arrives in front of the net and you race the goalie to get to it first—and you win. With the goalie far out of position, you may be able to net the ball with a light tap.

And there may be a time when you have a chance to receive a corner kick or crossing pass in front of the goal. Your role then is to head the ball into the net.

Whenever you shoot, have a target in mind. It's usually best to aim for a spot near the edge of the goal, two feet or so from the crossbar and one of the goalposts. Any shot toward the center of the goal is likely to be grabbed by the goalkeeper.

Low shots are likely to be the most troublesome for the goalie. He or she may have to dive to make the save. That's much more difficult than merely having to catch the ball or, in the case of a high shot, leap and nudge it over the crossbar.

And when you shoot, always charge in behind the ball. The shot may carom back off a post, the crossbar, the goalkeeper, or another of the opposition players. Or the goalie may bat the ball back. By following the shot, you'll be in a position to shoot a second time.

It may help you to be successful if you spend some time studying the goalkeeper during pre-game warm-ups. On what side does

Take the shot, then charge in behind it. The shooter here is UCLA forward Martin Bruno, who, with four goals, holds the Bruins' all-time single-game scoring record.

the goalie concentrate? Does the goalie dive for low balls to the right or left? Is the goalie aggressive about coming out to challenge shooters? Knowing the goalkeeper's strengths and weaknesses can be a big asset when the opportunity to shoot arrives.

Practice shooting with a teammate, drilling the ball back and forth. You can also practice in front of an empty net. Or you can practice against a wall or the side of a building. When you practice against a flat, upright surface, the ball is going to rebound back to you. Quickly get it under control and shoot again. You'll get many more chances to shoot than when you practice in front of an empty net and have to retrieve the ball after every shot.

The Tactical Game

Players on top-flight soccer teams, professional or amateur, are like wizards in the way they control the ball and move. Their passing is superb. They are bold and aggressive when they attack. Their defense is smoothly coordinated. Their goalkeeping is sure and confident.

When watching a polished team, it is difficult to believe that soccer once had about as much tactical savvy as a game of freeze tag. It was not a team sport as we know it today.

During the 1860s, soccer was known as "the dribbling game." Once a player got control of the ball, he—it was unthinkable that a woman would play the game—would try to dribble past as many players as he could toward the goal. When he eventually lost the ball, the player who recovered it would become the dribbler.

The 1870s brought an advance in strategy. Someone suggested that when a player had possession of the ball and was dribbling, a teammate might follow behind him, keeping alert to reclaim the ball should the dribbler lose it. This novel idea was called "backing up."

Even greater change came in 1872. Scotland played England in Glasgow, a game that ended in a scoreless tie. The English players returned home with exciting news. The Scottish team had used a style of play that was based on short passes along the ground.

Passing changed soccer drastically. One result was that it became much more of a team game.

No longer did players cluster around the ball like bees in a hive. Now they spread out, which made it easier to pass and receive passes. The era of positional play was dawning. Teams put a greater emphasis on formations, the way in which players are arranged on the field.

Formations are an important aspect of soccer today. They are defined by numbers. The order of numbers goes from defenders to midfielders to forwards. (The goalie is not included.)

The 4-3-3 Formation

In the 4-3-3 formation, there are four defensive players, three midfielders, and three forwards. Used frequently by high school and college teams, the 4-3-3 has been well known since 1962 when the Brazilian team used it in winning the World Cup.

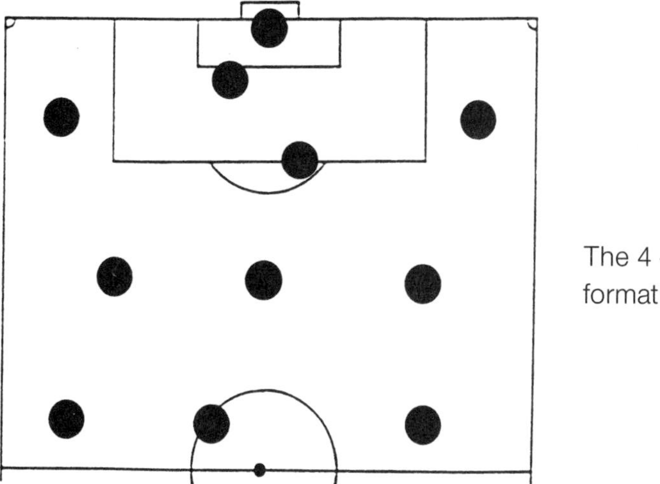

The 4 - 3 - 3 formation.

In the 4-3-3, the four defensive players are arranged in a diamond. The defender closest to the midfielders is called a stopper. The stopper is assigned to cover the opposition's center midfielder. The defender closest to the goal is called the sweeper. Often the sweeper is the best defensive player on the field.

The position of sweeper dates to 1947 and a small Italian soccer club named Triestina, which, at the time, was being thoroughly dominated by bigger, wealthier, more powerful clubs. In an effort to shut down goal-scoring thrusts by the rich clubs, Triestina began to position a fullback behind its other three defenders. The player's job was to cover the area in front of the goal. The player was called a *libero,* or free man.

Triestina enjoyed remarkable success with the new system and other teams adopted it. When teams in England copied this tactical change, they called the player a sweeper. The use of a sweeper has remained popular to this day.

The sweeper moves back and forth across the field, always following the ball and being alert to help out in covering any player who might slip past the other defenders. The sweeper also goes for loose balls near the goal.

The 4-4-2 Formation

With four defenders, four midfielders, and two forwards, the 4-4-2 formation is also popular today. It features more movement and shifting between the forwards and midfielders to create problems for the defense.

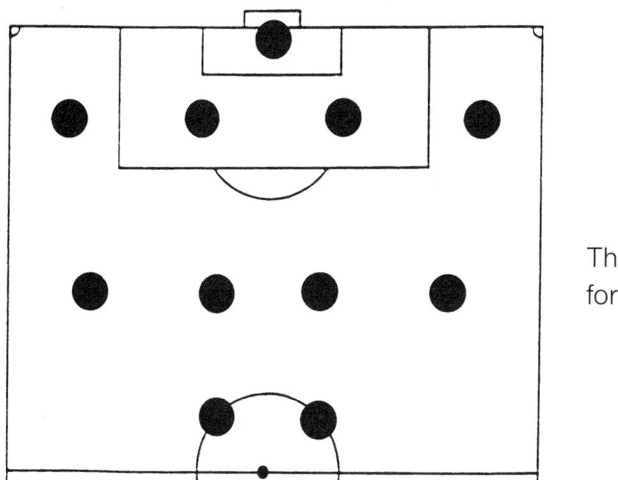

The 4 - 4 - 2 formation.

In the 4-4-2, the defense is composed of a stopper, a sweeper, and two wings. Their responsibilities are much the same as in the 4-3-3.

There's more pressure on the midfielders, however, who do a great deal of running. Either of the wing midfielders can play as forward, sprinting for the goal if an opening develops. The other wing then drops back to play a defensive role.

The center midfielders have greater defensive responsibilities in the 4-4-2. Each must cover his or her half of the field, taking over for the wing midfielders when they go on the attack.

The 3-5-2 Formation

With three defenders, five midfielders, and two forwards, the 3-5-2 provides much greater flexibility than the other formations.

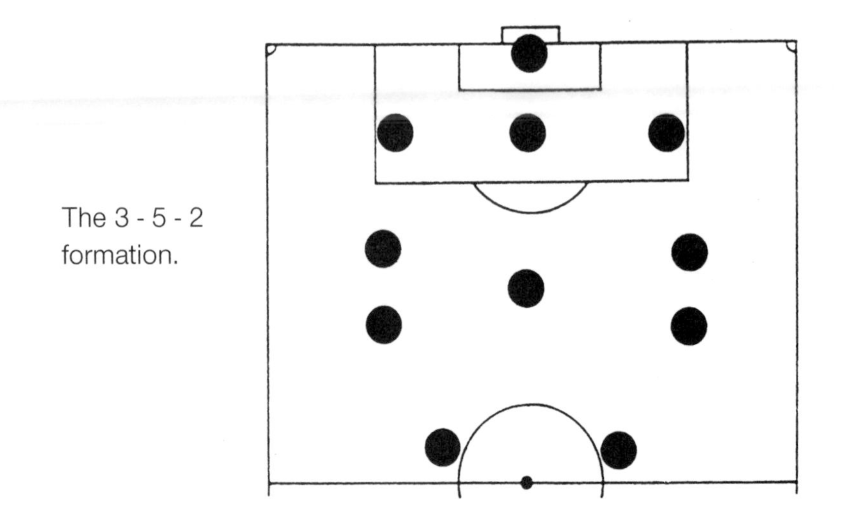

The 3 - 5 - 2 formation.

The defensive unit consists of two wing fullbacks and a sweeper. The fullbacks get help from two of the midfielders. The other three midfielders are free to play an attacking role.

The tactics a team uses are important, of course, but formations don't win games. It's the players working within the team's system that get results.

No matter what formation is being used, midfielders and forwards have to be flexible enough to help out on defense. Defenders must support the attack.

Understanding tactics and formations will give you an idea of how modern soccer is played. But you should concentrate on learning soccer's basic skills and having fun.

7

On Defense

In World Cup competition a number of years ago, Morocco faced a powerful West German team. Surprisingly, Morocco led, 1–0, at halftime. When the second half began, the Moroccan goalkeeper, Allal Ben Kassu, remained in the dressing room. Play got underway without him.

When Kassu finally showed up, he felt contrite for having let down his team. But his guilt quickly turned to embarrassment. When he glanced at the scoreboard, he saw that it was still 1–0. The Germans had not scored.

As Kassu surely learned that day, a strong defense can absolutely strangle an opposing attack. It does so by keeping the opposition from getting the ball. And if the offense does get it, the defense prevents the team from doing what it wants to do with it.

Most teams use a man-to-man system of defense. In this, you mark, or guard, a particular player. Less popular is the zone defense. When a team uses a zone, each player is assigned to cover a particular part of the field and any opponent who enters it.

No matter what system is used, good defense requires solid marking and tackling by team members. Both are vital.

Marking

When you move to mark an opponent with the ball, be sure to keep yourself positioned between the player and the goal. Keep well balanced. Bend slightly from the waist and at the knees. If the opponent changes direction, you want to be able to quickly react to that change.

How much space should there be between you and the opponent with the ball? It depends. Two or three yards are usually enough. But be prepared to give lots of room to any highly skilled player who's moving under a full head of steam.

If the opponent is dribbling toward you and traveling fast, don't make the mistake of lunging for the ball. The opponent is likely to simply dribble around you. Instead, move in close and force the opponent to slow down and change direction. You'll then be able to mark the player more closely.

If the opponent has no one to pass to, and you have a teammate backing you up, try tackling (see next page). Remember, however, that tackling can be risky. Again, you give your opponent a chance to elude you.

As this implies, playing defense requires teamwork. Defensive players should communicate with one another. Shout instructions to your teammates. Tell them whom to cover. If they get possession of a loose ball, tell them where to pass. Warn them of challenges.

In marking an opponent, your job is to follow the player wherever he or she goes.

Tackling

Tackling is using your feet to take the ball away from an opponent, usually when that player is not in full control of the ball. The opponent may have just received a pass, or perhaps allowed the ball to get well of ahead of his or her body.

• **FRONT TACKLE**—When you tackle an opponent straight on, keep your eyes on the ball. Be determined. Be confident that you're going to end up with the ball.

Lean forward. Concentrate your weight on your tackling leg. Use your shoulder to add authority to your move. Use the side of your foot to make contact with the ball.

When you move to tackle, keep your eyes on the ball; be aggressive.

- **TACKLING FROM THE SIDE**—You tackle from the side when you and your opponent with the ball are running side by side. Lean toward your opponent and use the outside of your foot to jab at the ball.

Again, use your shoulder. The rules permit shoulder charging. They say, however, that charging cannot be done "in a violent manner."

In attacking from the right or left, use your foot to try to flick the ball away.

- **SLIDING TACKLE**—You have to resort to a sliding tackle when an opponent with the ball has broken free and is heading for the goal. The sliding tackle can save the day. Come in fast from one side, fling your body to the ground feet first, and slide toward your opponent the way a runner in baseball slides into second base. Lash out with one foot to flick the ball away.

When attempting a sliding tackle, you cannot launch the move from behind the opposing player. That's a violation of the rules. The opposition gets an indirect free kick.

Be careful about timing your slide. If you slide too early, the opponent with the ball will simply swerve abruptly to the right or left and continue toward the goal.

Sliding too late is just as bad. You'll collide with the player who has the ball. The opposition will get a direct free kick.

The sliding tackle is often identified with soccer players from England, where damp and rainy days are common. Since British soccer is usually played on soft, grassy fields, sliding tackles are painless. But if your team plays on hard-packed dirt, you may want to limit your use of this tactic.

Defending on Dead Ball Plays

When the ball goes out of bounds across a sideline or over the goal line and a corner kick results, or when play is halted because of a foul and the ensuing free kick, the defense comes under added pressure. In such situations, the offense puts the ball in play; the defense can only react.

- **CORNER KICKS**—On corner kicks, the kicker usually sends a crossing pass several feet above the ground that travels parallel to the goal line. A member of the attacking team then tries to head the ball into the net.

When defending against this type of a play, the goalkeeper is the key player. The goalie should stand just inside the far post, ready to snatch the pass out of the air.

The kicker may be capable of launching an inswinger, a pass that curves toward the net. If an inswinger is expected, the goalkeeper should take up a position about midway in the goal. Another player should be stationed close to the near goalpost. Some teams also place a defender at the far post. Each of these players should shift over to protect a more central part of the goal should the goalkeeper dart forward to attack the crossing pass.

Each member of the defending team should mark an opposition player as the ball is being kicked. Take up a position between the player and the ball.

- **THROW-INS**—On short throw-ins, the player receiving the ball often tries to play the ball back to the thrower. To prevent this, a player should mark the thrower as soon as the ball is released.

Otherwise, throw-ins should be defended much as corner kicks. Each defender is assigned an attacker.

Long throw-ins are usually lofted high in the air. This gives the defenders a good chance of heading the ball into the clear.

- **FREE KICKS**—When indirect or direct free kicks are to be taken from within the penalty area, defensive players line up to construct a wall to protect the goal. The goalkeeper then covers the open area not screened by the wall.

The number of players used in forming the wall depends on the situation. When the kick is being taken from a central point near the penalty area, as many as five players might be used in the wall. A kick from a sharp angle at the side of the field probably requires only a two-player wall.

No matter the situation, the wall covers the side of the goal nearest to the ball. The goalie guards the open area.

A team's taller players are usually assigned to wall duty. They're better able to defend against a chip shot.

As a member of the wall, you have to be fearless. You have to be able to stand there and not duck or twist your body out of position as the kick is being taken. A ball that slips through the wall is a real threat, as dangerous as a shot that goes around it.

If the wall is successful in blocking the kick, immediately go on the attack. Your opponents will be out of position, committed to your team's half of the field. Now is the time to strike. Your forwards streak down the field. The midfielders get them the ball.

The World Cup

Since people around the world play the game, soccer is the only sport in which truly international tournaments are possible. Those tournaments take the form of the World Cup competition for men and women, held every four years.

To hundreds of millions of soccer fans in every corner of the globe, the World Cup matches trigger a special madness. Factories in Brazil shut down so that their workers can watch the Brazilian team on television. World Cup games have touched off border clashes between El Salvador and Honduras. When Saudi Arabia qualified for the Cup finals in 1994, a grateful nation gave each member of the squad parcels of land, bundles of cash, and a Mercedes.

The idea of bringing national soccer teams together in worldwide competition goes back about a century. To some extent, the Olympic Games satisfied that wish. Five teams competed in the first Olympic soccer tournament in 1908, and by 1924 the number increased to 22 teams. The United States took part for the first time that year.

But there was a problem with Olympic competition. Only amateur players were permitted to take part; professionals were banned.

This policy offended such European nations as England, Austria, Hungary, and the former Czechoslovakia, who allowed professionals to play on their national teams. These countries and others felt that they weren't being fairly treated by the Olympic organizers.

At this point, the Fédération Internationale de Football Association (FIFA) stepped forward, offering to create a men's world tournament for both amateurs and professionals. It would be scheduled every four years, between Olympic years. The first tournament was held in Uruguay in 1930.

The World Cup and the U.S.

More than 200 member nations of FIFA are eligible to take part in World Cup competition, but a tournament with anything approaching 200 teams would be difficult to manage and control.

Some weeding out is necessary. This process takes the form of qualifying rounds, which begin two years before the championship finals. The preliminary rounds determine which 30 teams will join the previous champion and the team representing the host nation in the final tournament. In 1998, 170 teams took part in 600 matches to decide the 32 qualifiers.

World Cup competition among the 32 finalists begins in June

Every four years, World Cup competition causes soccer mania. These are the championship trophies awarded men's and women's teams. (Men's trophy is at the left.)

and continues for about a month. The 32 teams are divided into eight groups. The four teams in each group all play one another. The two teams in each group who have the best record advance to the next round.

A single-elimination tournament reduces the number of teams from sixteen to eight. (Single elimination means one loss and a team is out.) Play then continues in the single-elimination format through the quarterfinals, semifinals, and finals.

Until competition was opened to women, the United States was seldom much of a factor in World Cup play. There were a few exceptions, however. In 1930, during competition for the first World Cup, an American team was one of the 12 to travel to Montevideo, Uruguay, for the finals. They were Americans in name only. The team was composed of English and Scottish professionals. By becoming American citizens, they made themselves eligible to represent the United States.

The American team defeated both Paraguay and Belgium by 3–0 scores to move into the semifinals. That was as far as they got. Argentina, the eventual tournament winner, eliminated the Americans, with the lopsided score of 6–1.

When the World Cup matches were held in Brazil in 1950, the United States, after a loss to Spain, faced England. The English, playing in World Cup competition for the first time, boasted two of the game's finest players. One was Stanley Matthews, a masterful dribbler and the most dangerous player of the time. The other was Tom Finney, described by soccer writer Paul Gardner as "perhaps the most complete all-around player ever to wear an England shirt."

Nobody gave the Americans a chance. They had played only two games together before arriving in Brazil. To Paul Gardner, they were "no hopers."

The English were so sure that they were going to win that they announced that Stanley Matthews would not play. He was to be rested for the more difficult matches that were to follow.

The game was played in Belo Horizonte, Brazil, under overcast skies. Incredibly, the Americans scored first. Several minutes before the first half ended, Haitian-born Joe Gaetjens dove for a crossing shot and headed it past the English goalkeeper. That goal was all that the Americans needed, for they held the English scoreless for the rest of the game.

Stanley Matthews watched from the sidelines, clenching his hands in frustration. So tightly did he clench them that he dug his fingernails into his palms without even realizing it.

Their shocking win over the British gave the Americans their only reason to celebrate. Shortly after, the team lost to Chile, 5–2, a defeat that ended their tournament participation.

At the 1990 World Cup in Rome, a team of young college players represented the United States. After a 5–1 thrashing at the hands of Czechoslovakia, the Americans reorganized and bolstered their defense in preparing to face Italy. While they were obviously overmatched by the competition, and were to lose, 1–0, they felt glad that they had "nearly tied" the skillful Italians.

In 1994, the United States played host to Cup competition for the first time. As the host nation, the United States qualified automatically for the 24-team finals.

In a major upset, the United States scored its first World Cup victory in 44 years by defeating Colombia, 2–1. America's first goal was scored when a Colombia defender, Andres Escobar, accidentally knocked the ball into his own net.

The United States faced soccer superstar Brazil in the second round. In the 74th minute of play, Brazil's Bebeto forced the ball past the upstretched fingers of the American goalkeeper for the game's only score. When the referee's whistle sounded, the joyous

FIFA WORLD CUP
FRANCE 98
19
adidas
FIFA WORLD CUP
FRANCE 98
20

Brazilians unfurled a huge American flag. It was a signal that the Americans deserved ranking as a world-class team.

In 1998, France became the first host nation since Argentina in 1978 to win the World Cup. For the United States, the 1998 tournament was a great failure. The Americans lost three games and won none, finishing dead last in the field of 32 finalists.

Since the men's tournament was first played, victorious nations have included the following:

1930: Uruguay
1934: Italy
1938: Italy
1950: Uruguay
1954: West Germany
1958: Brazil
1962: Brazil
1966: England
1970: Brazil
1974: West Germany
1978: Argentina
1982: Italy
1986: Argentina
1990: Germany
1994: Brazil
1998: France

Women and the World Cup

While American men have had only a handful of shining moments in World Cup play, it's been much different for American women. From the beginning, they performed with world-class brilliance.

FIFA introduced World Cup competition for women in 1991.

Brian Maisonneuve (left), a mainstay of the U.S. men's national team, duels for the ball in 1998 World Cup action.

China served as host for the first Women's World Cup. Twelve teams took part.

The American women were superb. They went unbeaten in their first five games in the two-week tournament. They then played Norway for the championship. The sprawling southern China city of Guangzhau played host. More than 65,000 fans packed the city's stadium.

The game was played evenly in the first half, with each team scoring one goal. Two minutes before the game's end, Michelle Akers stole a weak pass, dodged around the Norwegian goalie, and pushed the game winner into the net. With that goal, the American women laid claim to the nation's first championship in international soccer competition.

The American women were pioneers at the time. They had no role models, no female soccer stars that they could look up to. They were competing in a sport that was played chiefly by women in northern Europe and China.

When the American women returned to the United States from China and told others that they were world champions, they were often disappointed by their reactions. According to Carla Overbrook, captain of that World Cup team, a frequent response was, "We didn't even know you had a team."

Players on the team were mostly college students or recent graduates. One was a Stanford student who got her midterm exam by fax. The players didn't get paid and seldom saw their names in the newspapers. There were few television interviews and no endorsement opportunities.

Many players considered quitting, but there was talk that

women's soccer was going to become an Olympic sport. That was enough to persuade most team members to stick around.

In 1995, when the Women's World Cup tournament shifted to Sweden, the American women failed to live up to expectations. They lost to Norway, 1–0, in a semifinal match. Norway went on to win the Cup.

A tense moment for Mia Hamm (left) in the U.S.-Norway match during 1995 Women's World Cup competition.

That loss to Norway was a turning point for the American team. Out of the defeat came better days.

"A lot of things were not right about that team," forward Tiffeny Milbrett told *The New York Times*. "You have to be ready to give the best you have. In 1995, we weren't ready. Sometimes it takes a crisis to initiate change."

Tony DiCicco, who had become the team's head coach in 1994, made some tactical adjustments. The team had always used three defenders, which made it weak against counterattacks. DiCicco added a fourth defender. He also installed an intelligent, more determined attacking game.

Michelle Akers, who had scored 10 goals in Cup competition four years earlier, was moved from forward to defensive midfielder. Akers, at five feet, ten inches, would still be able to control a game with her superb tackling, heading, and passing skills.

"She's the best woman that's ever played the game," DiCicco said of Akers.

The rumors of women's soccer becoming an Olympic sport came true in 1996, and the United States women won the gold medal. After that, they became favored to regain their world championship. The tournament was to be played in the United States.

The women were fast, fit, smart, and experienced. The squad's average age was 24.5. Thirteen players were part of the 1996 Olympic team. Six were competing in their third World Cup. For six others, it was their second Cup competition. There were eight newcomers.

Originally, the plan was to play the tournament matches at small stadiums on the East Coast, but that was before the American women won the Olympic gold medal playing before 76,489 spectators at the University of Georgia. That outpouring convinced organizers to schedule matches at huge football stadiums.

The American team eased through the first round. They turned back Denmark, 3–0, then routed Nigeria, 7–1, scoring six goals in the first half. North Korea fell 3–0.

They defeated Germany, 3–2, in the quarterfinals, a victory that earned them a berth against Brazil in the semis. On the Fourth of July, they shut out the Brazilians, 2–0, at Stanford Stadium in Palo Alto, California. Five days later they played for the Cup. China provided the opposition.

Fast and technically skilled, China had defeated the Americans in two of three exhibition matches in 1999. They had downed powerful Norway, 5–0, in the other semifinal match.

"The two best teams made it to the finals," said Tony DiCicco. The game was played at the Rose Bowl in Pasadena, California, under blue skies and a glaring midday sun.

In the early stages, the United States team was unable to penetrate the tough Chinese defense. The Chinese, meanwhile, had problems with Michelle Akers, who controlled the center of the field, often outmuscling the smaller Chinese players. But Akers was knocked out of the game in the second half, suffering from dehydration and a bone-jarring collision with goalkeeper Briana Scurry that left her dazed. With Akers out of the game, the Chinese were able to attack with greater ease.

The game blazed through 90 minutes of regulation time with neither team scoring. Two 15-minute overtime periods followed, and still neither team could put the ball in the net.

With minutes to go in the second overtime period, on a corner kick, a Chinese forward sent the ball rocketing toward the left corner of the net. Midfielder Kristine Lilly was there. Positioned perfectly on the goal line, near the left post, she headed the ball

Michelle Akers played a vital role in the U.S. team's victory in the 1999 World Cup.

out of danger. Lilly, who would be named the game's Most Valuable Player, had taken away the best scoring opportunity either team had had.

A shootout eventually decided the game. Five players from each team were named to bang the ball 12 yards and past the opposition goalkeeper.

Said Briana Scurry, the U.S. goalkeeper: "I knew I had to make one save. Because my teammates would make their shots."

Scurry was right. She saved one Chinese player's shot. But all five of the American players—Carla Overbrook, Joy Fawcett, Kristine Lilly, Mia Hamm, and Brandi Chastain—came through.

Chastain's winner was a curling, left-footed shot just inside the left post. As it fell to the ground, Chastain stripped off her jersey and whirled it over her head as the fans erupted with thunderous cheers. The event is remembered as one of the greatest achievements in the history of women's sports.

The summer madness of 1999 served as another big boost for women's soccer, offering the promise of continued growth. Several years earlier, Joseph "Sepp" Blattner, FIFA's president, declared, "The future is feminine." Even Blattner could not have realized that the future would arrive so fast.

Soccer and the Olympics

The record of the United States in Olympic soccer is similar to the nation's performance in World Cup competition. American men have lagged behind their counterparts in many other countries of the world. American women, on the other hand, dazzled opponents and fans with their smart, aggressive play when women's soccer was introduced as an Olympic sport in 1996.

The Modern Games

The Olympic Games are the oldest of all truly international sports competitions. The ancient Olympics took place in Greece beginning in 776 B.C. and are believed to have continued every four years until A.D. 393.

What are called the modern games were first held in Athens, the capital of Greece, in 1896. With only a few breaks, they've been held continuously since then in various cities of the world at regular four-year intervals.

Soccer was not popular enough to be recognized as an official

Olympic sport in 1896. While it was offered as a demonstration sport at the Paris Olympics in 1900, it was not until 1908 that soccer became a full-fledged Olympic sport. It was, of course, a men's-only sport at the time.

Great Britain won the gold medal for soccer in 1908, defeating Denmark, 2–0. The British repeated four years later when the Olympics were held in Stockholm, Sweden.

Paris was the scene a second time in 1924, when the U.S. men made their debut in Olympic soccer competition. George Matthew Collins, a Boston newspaper columnist, coached the team. He trained his players on the deck of the passenger liner *America* during its trans-Atlantic voyage. Perhaps more training was needed, for the U.S. was bounced from the competition after its second game.

During the 1920s, 1930s, and into the 1940s, European nations were the Olympic soccer champions, except in 1924 and 1928 when Uruguay captured the gold medal. During the 1950s, eastern European nations began to dominate, a trend that continued until 1984 when the gold went to the French.

In 1960, with Olympic competition drawing more and more teams, regional qualifying rounds were established to decide which teams would meet in the finals. The United States achieved something of a breakthrough in 1972 by becoming one of the final 16 teams. The Games were held in Munich, Germany, that year. In the final matches, the United States tied one and lost two. The gold went to Poland.

In Australia in 2000, the American men did even better. With a 3–1 first-round victory over Kuwait, the United States surged into a berth in the quarterfinals for the first time. Although the

Americans lost to Chile, 2–0, they demonstrated that they were catching up to the rest of the world.

The win over Kuwait, however, was only the fifth Olympic victory for American men's soccer teams since 1924.

America's Claudio Reyna hurdles a downed player in a game against Portugal in the 1996 Olympics.

While Olympic soccer competition was originally limited to amateur players, the rules have been modified to admit professionals. There is an age restriction, however. Participants must be age 23 or under, but each team is allowed to carry three players older than 23.

Men's gold medal winners since 1908 were:

1908: England
1912: England
1916: (no competition)
1920: Belgium
1924: Uruguay
1928: Uruguay
1932: (no competition)
1936: Italy
1940: (no competition)
1944: (no competition)
1952: Hungary
1956: Soviet Union
1960: Yugoslavia
1964: Hungary
1968: Hungary
1972: Poland
1976: East Germany
1980: Czechoslovakia
1984: France
1988: Soviet Union
1992: Spain
1996: Nigeria
2000: Cameroon

Women's Competition

Unlike the American men, who would be happy to reach the second round of competition, U.S. women were favored to take the gold in the first Olympic women's competition in 1996.

As the players began making preparations for the event, the loss to Norway in World Cup competition the previous summer was still fresh in their memory. "That's something you never forget," said U.S. midfielder Julie Foudy. "It's etched in your brain every day."

Key additions to the squad included forwards Tiffeny Milbrett and Shannon MacMillan, and defender Brandi Chastain rejoined the team after a two-year absence. Coach Tony DiCicco also made tactical changes, discarding a 3-4-3 formation, which had become predictable, for a 4-4-2 and 3-5-2.

The U.S. team downed Denmark, 3–0, to advance to the semifinals against Norway. The two teams battled scorelessly for 90 minutes. Then, in the sudden-death overtime period, MacMillan blasted a low shot that beat the Norwegian goalkeeper and sent the U.S. into the gold medal match against China.

Forward Tiffeny Milbrett (right), a veteran performer with the U.S. women's national team, struggles for the ball during Olympic competition in 1996.

A record crowd of more than 76,000 filled the University of Georgia's Sanford Stadium in Athens, Georgia, for the match. The score was tied, 1–1, in the second half when Mia Hamm passed to Joy Fawcett, who set up Tiffeny Milbrett for the dramatic game-winning shot.

"This team is incredible," said Mia Hamm afterward. "I wouldn't trade this for anything in the world."

The women had made history in 1991 by winning the World Cup and achieving America's first triumph in the global soccer arena. Now they had won on an international level for the second time.

Mia Hamm looked upon that success as a victory not merely for her team but for all women athletes. She said: "With everyone embracing the women in these Olympic Games, we see it's all right [for women] to be successful. You gotta work hard, but the opportunities are there."

In the 2000 Olympics in Australia, the women were less successful than in 1996, losing to arch-rival Norway in the gold medal match. The 3–2 Norwegian victory came eleven minutes into overtime at Sydney Football Stadium before a crowd of 22,848.

The game marked the last time these American soccer heroes played together. In April 2001, a women's professional soccer league was scheduled to begin play, and many of the national team's brightest stars planned to join.

10

The Pros

When the United States was named to host World Cup competition in 1994, soccer officials in the United States pledged that they would form a world-class professional league. Major League Soccer, or MLS, a 12-team league that now operates from March through November, was the result.

Before Major League Soccer, more than a few attempts had been made to establish top-flight professional soccer in the United States.

The American Soccer League

The American Soccer League, founded in 1921, was the first pro league in the United States. It operated along the eastern seaboard. Teams were ethnic in character, reflecting American soccer's immigrant roots and its worldwide popularity.

In 1934, the Kearney (New Jersey) Irish won the league championship. In 1935, the Philadelphia Germans took the title; in 1943, the Brooklyn Hispanos were champions.

The American Soccer League established a number of soccer firsts during its years of operation. In 1937, the league introduced indoor soccer at New York's Madison Square Garden. In October 1952, it offered televised soccer for the first time, when station WPIX in New York carried an ASL game from Yankee Stadium.

During the 1960s, soccer managed to edge its way into the mainstream of American sports. New pro leagues were established in football, basketball, and hockey, as well as soccer.

The North American Soccer League

In 1967, a number of wealthy American businessmen formed not one, but two professional soccer leagues—the United States Soccer Association and the National Professional Soccer League. Both leagues' players came from world-class teams in Europe and South America.

Because of lack of fan support, neither league was successful. Millions of dollars went down the drain. In an effort to cut their losses, the owners of the two leagues agreed to unite into a single organization. Out of the merger came the 17-team North American Soccer League.

In the beginning, few fans attended NASL games. The league barely managed to stay alive. Twelve of the NASL's seventeen teams folded after the season of 1968.

Not until the mid-1970s did the NASL begin to show signs of success. New teams were added. In 1974, the NASL signed up its first West Coast franchise. By 1975, the league boasted 20 teams.

Yanks turn on power, but Mets still sputter
Page 67
POST SPORTS
MONDAY, AUGUST 15, 1977 25 CENTS
Jets snap slump, but Giants come up empty
Pages 62, 66
Cosmos thrill 77,691 fans

In I977 and 1978, the New York Cosmos of the old North American Soccer League drew record-breaking crowds. The league folded in 1985.

A chief reason attendance surged in 1975 was the signing of Pelé by the NASL's New York Cosmos. A forward, Pelé played the game with exceptional skill and creativity. He is recognized as the greatest soccer player in the history of the sport.

Pelé was his nickname. He was born Edson Arantes Nascimento. He was born on October 23, 1940, in the small Brazilian town of Tres Coracoes (Three Hearts).

Pelé's family was very poor. There was no money for soccer equipment. Pelé and his friends would get a man's sock, stuff it with rags or crumpled-up newspapers, form it into a ball shape, and tie it with string.

When he was 10, Pelé and some of his friends formed a soccer team. Unable to buy shoes, they played barefoot.

Pelé, who once described himself as being a "total failure" as a student, quit school to go to work in a shoe factory. When he wasn't working, he played soccer. When he was 14, he joined the adult team on which his father played.

Pelé's speed and elusiveness as a soccer player earned him a tryout with Santos, one of Brazil's most famous teams. He so impressed team officials that he was offered a contract with the Santos junior team. He was quickly promoted to the senior reserve team.

In 1958, not long before his 18th birthday, Pelé was chosen to play on Brazil's World Cup team. In a quarterfinal match against Wales, Pelé scored the game's only goal on a spectacular shot. With his back to the Welsh net, Pelé, using his right foot, hooked the ball back over his own head. When the ball caromed off the chest of a Welsh defender, Pelé spun around and, with his other foot, slammed the ball into the Welsh goal.

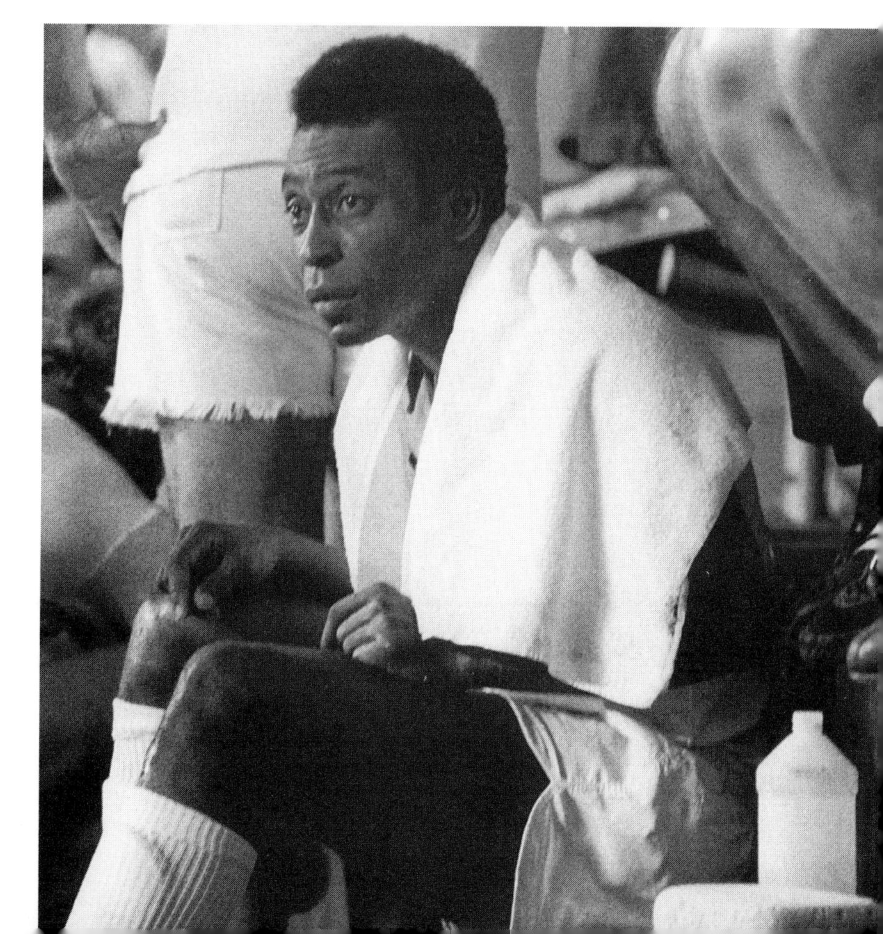

Anxious Pelé watches the Cosmos team from the sidelines.

Against France in the semifinals, Pelé's wizardry continued. He scored three goals, destroying the French team. Against Sweden in the finals, he scored the goal that brought Brazil its first World Cup. Pelé and the Brazilians went on to capture the World Cup again in 1962 and a third time in 1970.

Pelé was not big. He stood five feet, nine inches; he weighed about 165 pounds. He had massive thighs and a strong upper body. He was not only fast; he was very quick. From a standing start, he could be at full speed in two or three steps.

Pelé had amazing ball control skills. He could dribble through a cluster of several players, miraculously avoiding their frantic tackles. His passes were crisp and accurate.

His teammates and coaches praised him for his tactical ability. "A good player will be thinking two or three moves ahead," Gordon Bradley, coach of the Cosmos, once said, "but Pelé can think six or seven plays ahead."

For 15 years, Pelé reigned as soccer's standout player. Whenever he and the Santos team played exhibition games in the United States, they always drew huge crowds.

Pelé played his last game for Santos in 1974. He joined the New York Cosmos for the season that followed, signing a three-year contract worth $4.5 million.

Pelé has handclasps for young fans after a game at Giants Stadium in New Jersey.

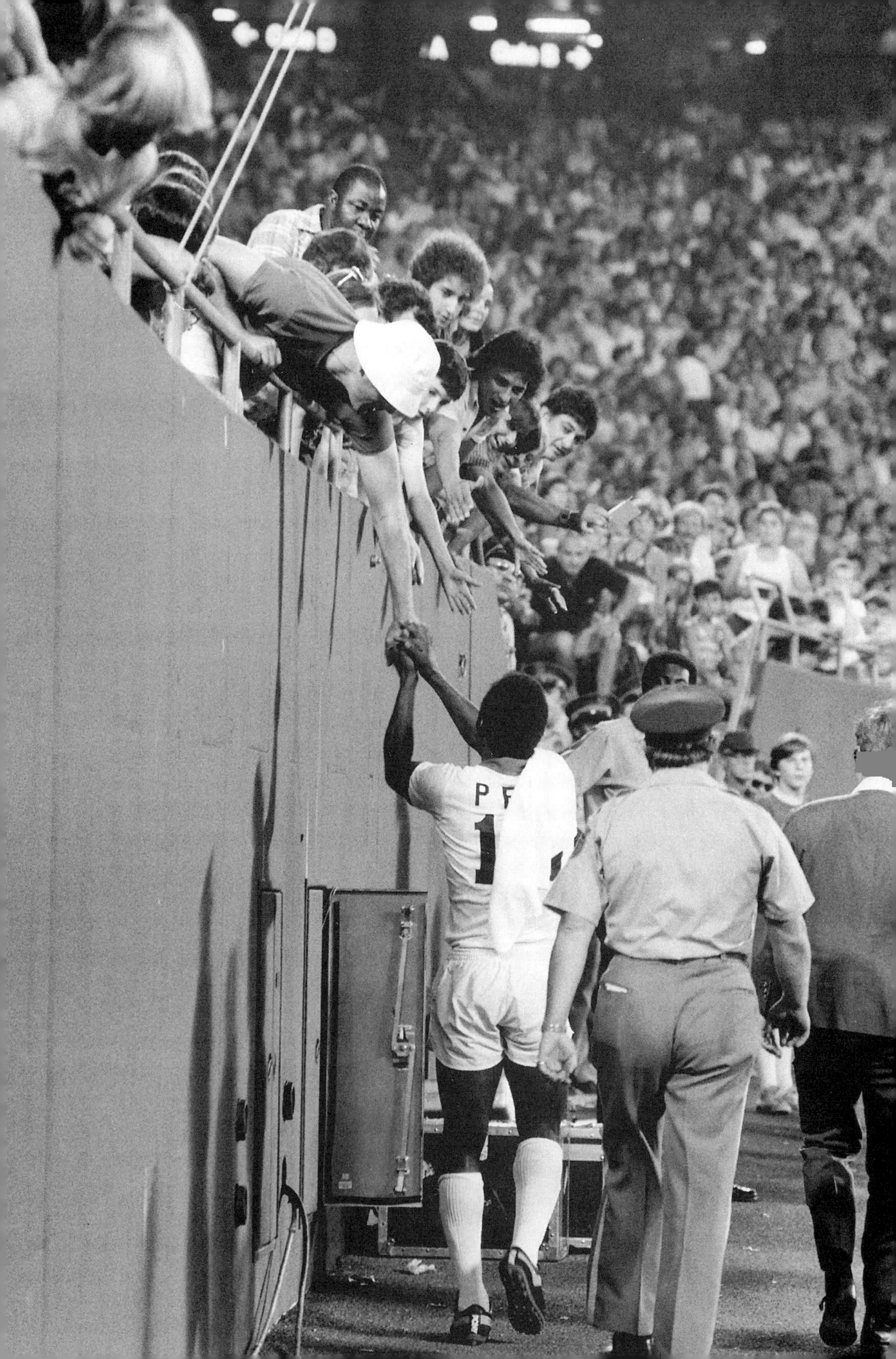

With Pelé, the NASL mushroomed in popularity. Capacity crowds greeted the Cosmos in Boston, St. Louis, San José, and many other league cities.

In 1977, the Cosmos began playing their home games at Giants Stadium in the Meadowlands of New Jersey, within sight of the Manhattan skyline. For a playoff game against Fort Lauderdale in 1978, a crowd of more than 78,000 poured into the stadium. Old-time soccer fans couldn't believe what was happening. ABC-TV began televising NASL games in 1979.

The Cosmos began to sign other internationally known stars. So did other NASL teams.

Some people were saying that soccer was now on the same level as baseball and football, but still there were problems. The international stars being signed by teams were demanding huge salaries. Teams were spending more money than they were taking in. The losses kept getting worse. In 1981, three NASL teams folded.

Other NASL teams moved from one city to another in search of success. Then they moved again. A team that began life as the Washington Darts in 1970 became the Miami Gators in 1971. The Gators then traveled several miles north in 1976 to emerge as the Fort Lauderdale Strikers. In 1984, the Strikers vaulted to the Midwest to be reborn as the Minnesota Strikers.

Other teams did much the same thing. With the continuous movement from one city to another, teams were unable to build a base of loyal fans.

More and more franchises went bankrupt. By 1983, the NASL was down to 12 teams. Three more teams dropped out after the season ended. In 1982, ABC-TV stopped televising games. In 1984, the league folded, as did the American Soccer League.

The NASL's collapse did not mean that professional soccer was finished in the United States—not at all. Smaller, mostly regional, leagues sprouted. The United States Inter-regional Soccer League, made up of some 40 soccer clubs, was the most important of these. The American Soccer League, formed in 1990 out of a merger of two other leagues, claimed to be "the only professional league in the United States sanctioned by the United States Soccer Federation."

None of the newly formed leagues proved to be of top-flight professional status. Major League Soccer, founded in 1995, would make that claim.

Major League Soccer (MLS)

When Major League Soccer set up shop, team owners sought to avoid the problems that undid the NASL. To curb overspending for players, MLS features what is a called a "single-entity" system of operation. Instead of a pro league made up of franchises owned by individuals, MLS has what are called investor-operators. Each has a financial stake in the league as well as in a particular team. Each investor-operator not only wants his or her team to do well, each also wants the league as a whole to be profitable.

Player contracts are issued by the league, not by individual teams. A team's general manager can scout players and recommend the ones that they want to sign, but if the players are believed to be too costly, the league will not approve them. The single-entity system of operation is also used by the Women's National Basketball Association, which is under the control of the NBA (National Basketball Association).

MLS began play as a 10-team league on April 6, 1996, with the San José Clash playing D.C. United. With the score tied at 0–0, and only two minutes remaining in the game, Eric Wynalda of the Clash scored the league's first goal, boosting the Clash to a 1–0 victory.

MLS expanded to 12 teams in 1998. Teams competed in three divisions:

EAST DIVISION	CENTRAL DIVISION	WEST DIVISION
D.C. United	Chicago Fire	Colorado Rapids
Miami Fusion	Columbus Crew	Kansas City Wizards
New England Revolution	Dallas Burn	Los Angeles Galaxy
MetroStars (New York)	Tampa Bay Mutiny	San José Clash

When it comes to soccer stadiums, the home grounds of the Columbus (Ohio) Crew are considered the standard of excellence.

Eventually, MLS expects to be a 16-team league. Such cities as Charlotte, Seattle, Cleveland, Philadelphia, San Diego, Houston, and Atlanta have expressed interest in acquiring MLS teams.

A point system is used in helping to determine which teams will be included in the playoffs. During the regular season, a team gets three points for a win in regulation or overtime, and the loser none. If the game ends in a tie, each team earns one point.

In the MLS's first four years, the league decided tie games with a shootout (as in World Cup play). In a shootout, five players from each team alternately take penalty shots against the opposition team's goalie. The team scoring the most penalty shots wins. Beginning with the season of 2000, the league eliminated the shootout in favor of a 10-minute sudden-death overtime, divided into two halves, to decide a tie. If neither team scores during the overtime, the game is recorded as a tie.

The winners of each division and the five teams with the best records, no matter their divisions, compete in the playoffs. The two best teams as determined by the playoffs compete for the MLS Cup.

Project 40

A joint venture between MLS and the U.S. Soccer Federation, Project 40 provides valuable training and experience for some of America's best college players. It's also a means of developing home-grown stars.

It's called Project 40 because it singles out 40 college players and arranges at least 40 games for each of them. Players get intensive training from professional coaches and occasionally play in MLS games for the pro team they represent.

Each Project 40 player earns the minimum MLS salary. As a result, the National Collegiate Athletic Association (NCAA) considers Project 40 players to be professionals. They therefore could lose whatever scholarships they might have received from their school.

The U.S. Soccer Federation solved this problem. The organization offers Project 40 participants a five-year tuition scholarship if they do not continue in the pro ranks.

Instead of playing solely on a college team, Project 40 participants get a taste of what it is like to compete as a professional. They develop at a faster pace as a result.

D.C. United

During MLS's first four years of operation, D.C. United was the league's dominant team. D.C. United competed in all four title games, winning three of them. The only time D.C. United lost was to the Chicago Fire in 1998.

Marco Etcheverry, the league's best playmaker, sparked D.C. United's attack. For example, in a semifinal game against Columbus in 1999, Etcheverry, from Bolivia, set up three goals and scored one himself in D.C. United's 4–0 win. Alex Yannis, veteran soccer writer for *The New York Times*, called Etcheverry "unstoppable" in big games.

D.C. United's consistent success in MLS playoffs may not have been the team's most notable achievement. In Inter-American Cup competition in 1998, D.C. United captured a two-of-three game series from Vasco da Gama, the legendary Brazilian club. The stunning victory sent shock waves through the international soccer world.

Following D.C. United's win over the Los Angeles Galaxy for the league title in 1999, a victory parade and rally were held in Washington for the team. But only a few thousand Washingtonians turned out.

The D.C. United players were easy to approach and speak to. They smiled, shook hands, and signed autographs. There was no great crush of fans around them. "This is a sign," noted *The Washington Post,* "that soccer has not yet arrived and Washington doesn't yet know what it has."

2000 and Beyond

As the new millennium began, professional soccer in the United States was still working hard to gain broad-based acceptance. The hope, of course, is that one day the league will attain a level of popularity on a par with Major League Baseball, professional football, or NBA basketball. That goal is not close to being achieved. The average attendance per game, about 17,000, is below expectations. As of 1999, no MLS team had shown a profit.

But through its training programs and by virtue of the career opportunities it offers young players, MLS is playing a vital role in elevating the level of play of American soccer. In this respect, at least, the league can be called a success.

11

Looking Back

Where was soccer first played? It's impossible to say.

Sports historians can cite the names of the individuals who "invented" basketball or volleyball, and the beginnings of baseball and football are pretty well established, but it's different with soccer. It's probably because the idea of kicking a round object is not very inventive. It's like the first time someone hit a ball with a stick or people wrestled—such events could have happened any place at any time.

One thing is certain: Soccer is one of the oldest sports in the world. Throughout most of recorded history, different cultures are known to have played games in which a ball, or something resembling a ball, was kicked with the feet.

Huang-Ti, a Chinese emperor who reigned almost 4,000 years ago, is said to have created *tsu-chu,* a game played with the feet by opposing teams using a leather ball stuffed with hair and cork.

The ancient Greeks played a game called *episkiros* that involved kicking and throwing a ball within an open area marked off with boundary lines.

The Romans copied that kicking-throwing game and called it *harpastum.* It became popular with Roman foot soldiers. When the Romans occupied England, the legionnaires took the game with them. Legend has it that English residents of the town of Derby defeated a team of Roman soldiers in this early version of soccer in A.D. 276.

The game grew rapidly in England. Often boys and men of one village competed against those of another. There was no field with carefully laid out boundary lines. Instead, the idea was to boot the ball cross-country into the opponent's village.

By the 14th century, the game had become so popular that it was considered a menace. At the time, England's King Edward III was locked in a struggle to take over France. The king felt that his men were spending too much time playing "skittles, quoits, fives, football [soccer], or other foolish games." He wanted them to practice instead with their bows and arrows. He threatened to toss them into jail unless they got more serious about archery.

Soccerlike games continued to grow in popularity. One version allowed players to run while holding the ball. (This was to become

During the 1700s, one version of soccer was played on an oval-shaped court.

the sport of rugby.) Another set of rules stated that the ball could only be advanced with the feet, that is, by dribbling. Still another version permitted kicking an opponent's legs, a tactic known as shinning or hacking.

The different forms of the sport continued until well into the 19th century. On December 8, 1863, England's newly formed Football Association, made up of clubs in London and neighboring communities, announced an official set of rules. "No player shall run with the ball," said one of the rules. "No tripping or kicking shall be allowed," declared another.

Not only did the Football Association establish the official rules of soccer, but the organization also gave the game its name: Association Football. The word *soccer* comes from the word *association*, or from *assoc.*, the abbreviated form of it.

An International Sport

Soccer became widely popular in England. The nation was one of the world's great commercial powers at the time. English soldiers, sailors, and colonizers transported soccer to every corner of the globe. The game grew quickly throughout Europe and South America.

The Fédération Internationale de Football Association (FIFA) was formed in 1904. France, Belgium, Switzerland, Holland, Sweden, Spain, and Denmark were the original members. FIFA helped to make the rules of soccer the same all over the world. A team from Norway, for example, could oppose one from Argentina, and could be sure that each was playing exactly the same game. And competing in soccer gave different teams a sense of the world community of nations.

Soccer was slow to develop in the United States. The Boston Oneidas, the first organized soccer club in America, was formed in 1862. From 1862 to 1865, the Oneidas, playing other amateur teams, went undefeated. A plaque in Boston Common, where the team played its home games, commemorates that achievement.

During the final decades of the 19th century and the early years of the 20th century, waves of immigrants from Europe flooded into the United States, and they brought soccer with them. Teams and leagues sprang up in immigrant neighborhoods. They carried such names as the Brooklyn German-Americans, New York Ukrainians, Hartford Italians, Chicago Slovaks, and Cleveland Shamrocks.

College Soccer

The history of college soccer goes back about a century. Several colleges and universities played soccer before 1900, but no governing body existed until the Intercollegiate Association Football League was organized in 1926. Members included Columbia, Cornell, Harvard, Pennsylvania, and Haverford.

The colleges tinkered with the rules a bit. They played the game in four quarters instead of two halves. They replaced the throw-in with a kick-in. And the colleges allowed free substitution, whereas the official rules didn't permit any substitution at all.

Under the college rules in effect today, up to 18 players can be used in a game, meaning that seven are substitutes. Permitting all those substitutions changes the character of the game. A player can be sent into a game, play all-out for 10 or 15 minutes, be taken out to rest, and then put back in again.

This makes college soccer more of a power game; there's less emphasis on skill.

It also expands the role of the coach during a game. He or she is more like a coach in basketball, constantly sending in substitutes and making decisions that affect how the game is being played. The role of each player is reduced.

Despite these changes, college soccer enjoyed a period of rapid growth during the 1960s. By the 1970s, the National Collegiate Athletic Association (NCAA) had sanctioned hundreds of soccer programs.

The NCAA established championship competition for college soccer in 1959. Saint Louis University dominated the tournament in its early years. The University of Virginia reigned as champion from 1990 to 1994. Indiana University won in 1998 and repeated in 1999.

The NCAA introduced a championship tournament for women in 1982. North Carolina captured the title that year. In the years that followed, the Tar Heels kept winning and winning. When North Carolina captured the title in 1999 with a 2–0 victory over Notre Dame, it marked the 15th national championship for the team in 18 years.

Soccer's growth as a college sport continues. By 2000, there were more than 1,400 four-year colleges with men's and women's soccer programs. And the men's and women's college championships, held each November and December, earned television coverage and big, bold headlines in newspapers from one coast to another.

Soccer Today

Soccer got off to a slow start in the United States, but in the last few decades the sport has grown at a rapid rate. The women's national team, playing intelligent, entertaining soccer, triggered the most recent surge in the game's popularity. "We want to show the world that we're excellent soccer players—fit, fast, athletic—and that we have everything the men's game does," forward Tiffeny Milbrett told *The New York Times* not long before the women's World Cup victory in 1999. "We want respect."

The team got just that. Through their winning performances, the team has helped women's soccer to achieve a level of success never dreamed of. Among young girls in suburban America, soccer flourishes as no other sport.

Today, youth soccer is everywhere in the United States. College soccer continues to grow by leaps and bounds. Major League Soccer, the No. 1 professional league in the United States, has gained respectable status.

When the World Cup competition was telecast for the first time in the United States in 1966, it created the first burst of interest in the sport. It has grown in spurts since that time. Soccer in the United States may not yet be a big-time professional sport like baseball or football, but tens of millions of Americans take pleasure in the sport just the way it is.

Soccer Words and Terms

BACK—A defensive player. Backs are usually assigned to cover forwards.

BREAKAWAY—A game situation in which a player in possession of the ball, having cleared the last of the defensive players, bears down on the goal.

BOX—The penalty area; also called the 18-yard box.

CENTER—To pass the ball into the penalty area from an area near one of the sidelines.

CHARGE—The legal use of the shoulder to push an opposing player off balance.

CLEAR—To kick or head the ball up the field, away from the goal one is defending.

CORNER KICK—A free kick given to the attacking team from the corner area after a defensive player has driven the ball beyond his or her own goal line.

DEAD BALL—A ball that is temporarily out of play.

DEFENDER—A member of the last line of defense in front of the goalkeeper.

DIRECT FREE KICK—A free kick awarded a team after a foul. A goal may be scored directly from the kick.

DRIBBLING—Moving or advancing the ball along the ground with a series of light kicks.

DROP KICK—The method used by the referee to restart the game after a temporary suspension of play (as when a player had been injured or two opponents have knocked the ball out of bounds simultaneously). The ball is dropped between two opposing players, each of whom tries to kick or gain control of it.

END LINE—Either of two lines at the extreme ends of the playing field; the goal line.

FORWARD—A member of the attacking line.

FULLBACK—A defender.

GOAL AREA—The rectangle, six yards by twenty yards, directly in front of the goal.

GOALKEEPER—A team's last line of defense. He or she keeps the ball from going into the goal for a score.

GOAL KICK—The free kick awarded the defensive team when the attacking team kicks the ball over the goal line.

GUARD—To mark; to act to prevent an opponent from playing effectively or scoring.

HALF VOLLEY—A kick made just as the ball bounces.

HANDBALL—Touching the ball with any part of the hands or arms.

HEADER—To play the ball with the forehead with the intention of passing, shooting, or clearing it.

HEAD SHOT—A header that is intended as a scoring effort.

INDIRECT FREE KICK—A free kick awarded a team after a foul. At least two players must touch the ball before a goal can be scored.

JUGGLE—To keep the ball in the air without using your hands.

KICKOFF—The method of putting the ball in play at the start of the game or after a goal has been scored. From the center circle, a player passes the ball to a teammate.

LINESMAN—An official who assists the referee, usually working along a sideline to indicate when the ball or a player with the ball is out of bounds. The linesman normally awards throw-ins, corner kicks, and goal kicks.

MARK—To guard an opponent.

MIDFIELDER—A player who plays in the center of the field, between the forwards and backs.

OBSTRUCTION—A foul that occurs when a player deliberately runs in the path of an opponent who is attempting to reach the ball; an indirect free kick is awarded to the opposing team.

OFFSIDE—A rule stating that when a player is about to receive a pass from a teammate, the player must have two opposing players closer to the goal than he or she is. (One of the opposing players is normally the goalie.)

PENALTY AREA—The rectangle, 18 yards by 44 yards, in front of each goal.

PENALTY KICK—A free kick that is awarded a team that has been fouled within the penalty area.

RED CARD—The card that is used to signal to a player that he or she is being ejected.

REFEREE—The official in charge. The referee starts the game and serves as official timekeeper, calls fouls, and is empowered to caution players or eject them from the game.

SCREEN—To maintain control of the ball by keeping the body between the ball and an opposing player.

STRIKER—A forward whose chief task is to score goals.

SWEEPER—A defender who roams free in support of other defenders and to handle loose balls.

TACKLE—To use the feet in an attempt to take the ball away from an opponent.

THROW-IN—To toss the ball back into play after it has gone out of bounds. The throw-in is a two-handed over-the-head throw, with the thrower standing outside the field of play.

TRAP—To bring the ball under control.

VOLLEY—A kick made while the ball is in the air.

WALL—A line of players used to defend against a free kick.

YELLOW CARD—The card used to signal a warning to a player that further misconduct can result in his or her ejection.

For More Information

Soccer is one of the most organized of all American sports. There are associations and federations that pertain to every aspect of the game. They serve the boys and girls who play the game and their parents; adult players, both amateur and professional, at every skill level; and coaches, referees, and administrators. These organizations include:

AMERICAN YOUTH SOCCER ORGANIZATION (AYSO)

12501 South Isis Avenue, Hawthorne, CA 90250

PHONE: (310) 643-6455 • FAX: (310) 640-5310

WEBSITE: http://www.soccer.org

Founded in California in 1964 with the goal of assisting parents, coaches, and communities in the development of young soccer players, the AYSO now offers programs for boys and girls from ages four through eighteen in nearly every state. Its 250,000 volunteer coaches, referees, and administrators serve a membership of approximately 700,000 players. "Everyone plays," is the AYSO philosophy; skill level is not a criterion for participation. AYSO publications include "The ABCs of AYSO," "Parents' Handbook," "Soccer Now," the largest circulation soccer publication in the U.S., "In Play," a quarterly publication for coaches and referees, and "Tournament Talk," a monthly listing of AYSO tournaments.

THE CANADIAN SOCCER ASSOCIATION (CSA)

237 Metcalfe Street, Ottawa, Ontario K2P 1R2
PHONE: (613) 237-7678 • FAX: (613) 237-1516
WEBSITE: http://www.canoe.ca/soccer

Similar to the U.S. Soccer Federation, CSA is the governing body of soccer in Canada. The organization supervises international competition, professional leagues, and national championships, and administers a wide range of other programs vital to the sport.

FÉDÉRATION INTERNATIONALE DE FOOTBALL ASSOCIATION (FIFA)

Hitzigweg 11, 8030 Zurich Switzerland
WEBSITE: http://www.fifa.com

Founded in 1904 to establish soccer's official rules and provide unity among national soccer associations, FIFA today is an organization of 203 members, making it the largest organization of its type in the world. Besides sponsoring the World Cup for both men and women, FIFA oversees Olympic soccer competition and sponsors several other international tournaments, including the World Youth (under 20) Championship, the Futsal (Indoor Football) World Championship, the Under-17 World Championship, and the Confederations Cup competition.

INTERCOLLEGIATE SOCCER ASSOCIATION OF AMERICA (ISAA)

4301 Broadway Street, San Antonio, TX 78209-6318

Affiliated with the NCAA and the U.S. Olympic Committee, ISAA promotes soccer participation on a college level. The organization calculates weekly ratings of college teams, selects men's and women's All-American teams, and names championship teams in eight regions of the United States.

MAJOR LEAGUE SOCCER (MLS)

110 East 42nd Street, New York, NY 10017
PHONE: (212) 450-1200 • FAX: (212) 450-1300
WEBSITE: http://www.MLSNET.com

Founded in 1996, MLS is America's principal professional soccer league. It is made up of twelve teams in three conferences, with each team playing a 32-game schedule in a season that stretches from March into November. The regular season is followed by playoffs to determine the MLS champion. Also active in the development of young players, MLS supervises the operation of more than a thousand soccer camps for young players between the ages of five and eighteen.

NATIONAL INTERCOLLEGIATE SOCCER OFFICIALS ASSOCIATION (NISOA)

541 Woodview Drive, Longwood, FL 32779-2614
PHONE: (407) 862-3305 • FAX: (407) 862-8545

A membership organization for more than 4,000 high school and college soccer referees, NISOA sponsors regional officiating clinics, produces audiovisual instructional aids, and operates summer training camps and a soccer officials' hall of fame.

NATIONAL SOCCER COACHES ASSOCIATION OF AMERICA (NSCAA)

6700 Squibb Road, Suite 215, Mission, KS 66202-3252
PHONE: (913) 362-1747 • FAX: (913) 362-3439
WEBSITE: http://www.nscaa.com

A membership organization of approximately 15,000 soccer coaches,

NSCAA provides educational information, sponsors coaching clinics, conducts an awards program, including the "Coach-of-the-Year" selection. The organization is affiliated with the NCAA and U.S. Soccer Federation.

NATIONAL SOCCER HALL OF FAME

18 Stadium Circle, Oneonta, New York 13820
PHONE: (607) 432-3351 • FAX: (607) 432-3645
WEBSITE: http://www.soccerhall.org

"This is the first sports museum dedicated to soccer," says Will Lunn, Hall of Fame President. Besides the museum and the Hall of Fame itself, the complex offers a library, Hall of Fame store, administrative offices, and a special "Kicks Zone" where visitors can test their soccer skills.

SOCCER ASSOCIATION FOR YOUTH (SAY)

4050 Executive Park Drive, Suite 100, Cincinnati, OH 45241
PHONE: (513) 769-3800 • FAX: (513) 769-0500
WEBSITE: http://www.saysoccer.org

A membership organization for boys and girls ages four through eighteen that is part of the USSF family, SAY (also known as SAY Soccer) seeks to assure maximum participation in soccer without concern for skill levels. SAY prescribes soccer rules, forms leagues, sanctions local and state tournaments, and offers clinics for coaches and referees. The organization also provides discounts on soccer merchandise.

UNITED STATES SOCCER FEDERATION (USSF)

1801–1811 S. Prairie Avenue, Chicago, IL 60616
PHONE: (312) 808-1300 • FAX: (312) 808-1301
WEBSITE: http://www.us-soccer.com

The governing body of soccer in the United States, USSF is made up of state organizations that represent approximately three million individual members. The organization provides the official rules of play, registers teams and leagues, sponsors 11 national tournaments, and conducts training programs for the licensing of coaches and referees. USSF publishes booklets titled "FIFA Laws of the Game" and "Guide for Referees."

UNITED STATES FUTSAL FEDERATION (USFF)

P. O. Box 40077, Berkeley, CA 94704-4077
PHONE: (510) 334-8733 • FAX: (510) 527-8110
WEBSITE: http://futsal.com

An affiliate of the U.S. Soccer Federation, USFF is the governing body of futsal in the United States. (Futsal is the only version of indoor soccer approved by FIFA.)

UNITED STATES YOUTH SOCCER ASSOCIATION (USYSA)

899 Presidential Drive, Suite 117, Richardson, TX 75081
PHONE: (972) 235-4499 • FAX: (214) 235-4480
WEBSITE: http://www.usysa.org

The youth division of the U.S. Soccer Federation and the largest organization in the United States devoted to the development of young soccer players, USYSA has more than three million members between the ages of five and nineteen, 600,000 volunteer workers, and 300,000 coaches. USYSA assists in the organization of leagues, supervises state, regional, and national tournaments, conducts workshops on coaching, refereeing, and league administration, and publishes "USYSA Newspaper," a quarterly publication for coaches, referees and administrators.

Index